THE GIRLS OF CANBY HALL

PRINCESS WHO?

EMILY CHASE

No part of this publication may be reproduced in whole or in part, or stored in a retrieval system, or transmitted in any form or by any means, electronic, mechanical, photocopying, recording, or otherwise, without written permission of the publisher. For information regarding permission, write to Scholastic Inc., 730 Broadway, New York, NY 10003.

ISBN 0-590-41055-7

Copyright © 1987 by Scholastic Inc. All rights reserved. Published by Scholastic Inc. THE GIRLS OF CANBY HALL is a trademark of Scholastic Inc.

SCHOLASTIC INC.
New York Toronto London Auckland Sydney

ISBN 0-590-41055-5

12 11 10 9 8 7 6 5 4 3 2 1   7 8 9/8 0 1 2/9

Printed in the U.S.A.   01

First Scholastic printing, October 1987

THE GIRLS OF CANBY HALL

PRINCESS WHO?

THE GIRLS OF CANBY HALL

CHAPTER ONE

Jane Barrett pushed a strand of long blonde hair behind her ear, took a firm grip on the yellow marker she used for highlighting, opened her history book, and ordered herself to concentrate.

Fifteen seconds later, she was staring out the window again. It was so beautiful outside; the campus of Canby Hall, a private girls' high school in Greenleaf, Massachusetts, looked its best on spring days like this — the grass was velvety green, the flower beds were rainbows of color, and the huge old trees made nice shady places to bring a book and study.

Except that Jane couldn't study under a tree. She'd tried it once, and it was awful. Leaves kept dropping onto her book, and ants kept crawling up her ankles. Jane needed a quiet place with a desk and a good chair to study in. The problem was she had it — right here in Room 407 of Baker House — but it wasn't doing her any good. Final exams were coming up, and she knew she'd have to work hard to stay on the honor roll, but she just couldn't concentrate.

She glanced guiltily at her book and then let her gaze wander across the room. One of her two roommates, Toby Houston, was sitting cross-legged on her bed, chewing on a pencil and frowning at her geometry book. Her curly red hair was in corkscrews from being twisted around her finger, and her green eyes were squinting as she tried to get her mind around some tricky problem.

Toby's side of the room was very different from Jane's, which had an antique quilt on the bed and a Persian rug in muted tones of blue and gray on the floor. In contrast, Toby's bed had a bright rainbow comforter with matching pillows on it, pictures of her father and her horse, Max, back in Texas were on her desk, and a single tea bag was taped to the ceiling above. No one knew what the tea bag was for, and Toby wasn't talking.

At least the rainbows were an improvement, Jane thought with a smile. When Toby had first arrived, she hadn't decorated her side of the room at all, except for the pictures and the tea bag. And she'd wrapped herself in some faded old army blanket and slept on top of the sheets, like she was out on the open range around a campfire.

The third person in Room 407, Andrea

Cord, who was from Chicago, *did* decorate her part of the room. Unfortunately, as far as Jane was concerned, it was with a matching bedspread and throw rug in diagonal earth-tone stripes. They went with the soothing Wedgwood blue walls, which Jane had painted, about as well as the bright primary colors of Toby's rainbows.

When Jane had first moved into 407, she'd hoped to have the room all to herself and to decorate it tastefully, like her own room in Louisburg Square in Boston. She didn't get what she'd hoped for; instead she got something better — two of the best friends she'd ever had. Now if she could just study, things would be almost perfect.

Suddenly, Toby dropped her geometry book and flopped back on the bed. "Yucch!" she said to the tea bag.

"I agree," Jane told her. "It's been here since September. It's probably moldy and covered with dust. It's time to tell us what it's for and then banish it from Room 407 forever."

Toby lifted her head off the pillow and grinned. "Not a chance," she said. "Anyway, I wasn't talking about the tea bag. I was talking about geometry. I'll never get good at it."

"You're just not concentrating."

"Neither are you," Toby pointed out. "You've been staring around the room and out the window for ten minutes straight."

"I know, I know!" Jane sounded slightly frantic. "I've never had trouble studying before. I just don't understand it."

"It's the weather," Toby said. "Everybody gets a little loco in the springtime."

"Loco?" Jane said. "I suppose that's a Texas term for crazy?"

"You got it," Toby told her. "Straight from Rattlesnake Creek. Actually, it's Spanish. We Texans just adopted it."

"Well, I'm not loco," Jane said. "Not yet, anyway. But I will be if I don't get some work done."

"Right," Toby agreed, sitting up and opening her book again. She worked for ten minutes, managed to understand the problem, and looked up happily to tell Jane. But Jane was staring out the window again.

Without a word, Toby got off her bed and waded through the piles of clothes that Jane had the habit of leaving on the floor. Reaching up, she pulled the window shade down with a snap, took a silk scarf and a pair of knee socks off of Jane's study lamp, and turned it on.

"Pretend it's night," she said, going back to her bed and turning on her lamp. "Pretend it's the middle of the night and tomorrow's your history final."

Amazingly, it worked, and for almost an hour, Room 407 was quiet except for the scratching of Toby's pencil and the slight squeak of Jane's yellow marker. Both girls were concentrating so well that they didn't even hear Andy until she was inside the room.

"What's this?" Andy asked. "Did somebody die or something?" She set a cardboard box down on the floor and stood with one hand on her hip. "This place is so gloomy I feel like I'm at a funeral."

"We couldn't study and Toby came up with the bright idea of making it feel like nighttime," Jane explained, "and it worked."

"Whatever keeps you going, I guess," Andy commented. Picking up the box, she went over to her part of the room, which was different from Jane's in more than just decor. There were no piles of clothes on the floor, no papers scattered on the desk and the bed, no empty cracker wrappers, and no dustballs. Everything was clean and neat and in its place, just the way Andy liked it.

Opening the box, Andy lifted out wads of newspaper, and then a smaller box tied with string. "Hope I'm not making too much noise," she said.

"No, that's okay," Jane told her, eyeing the box and then quickly going back to her book.

"You're sure?" Andy asked, a teasing smile on her lips.

"Can't hear a thing," Toby said, also sneaking a look at the box.

"Well, that's good." Andy's smile was bigger now, and as she dug into the box, a sweet, enticing aroma wafted into the room.

In a few seconds, both Jane and Toby were sniffing the air. "I don't believe it, Andrea Cord!" Jane said. "You got a care package from home, and you're going to sit there and eat it right in front of us!"

Andy's care packages were famous in Baker House. Her parents owned and ran a restaurant in Chicago. Even though they still had three children at home, they missed Andy. They regularly sent the care packages — batches of cookies, loaves of homemade bread, pans of fudge. This time it was caramel corn, fresh and crisp and generously drizzled with sweet, sticky caramel.

"Would I do anything as mean as eating this without sharing it?" Andy asked, pretending to be insulted. "I came up the stairs all ready to pass it around, but you two were so busy studying in your dark little cave that I just didn't want to disturb you. Maybe I should go out into the hall or down to the kitchen."

"Don't you dare!" Jane cried.

"Anywhere that box goes, we go!" Toby added, scrambling off her bed.

Andy laughed and held out the box. "Help yourselves," she said. "After all, what kind of friend would I be if I didn't let you fill up with this before dinner?"

"Uh-oh." Jane stopped in mid-munch. "You've seen the menu."

Andy nodded.

"What is it tonight?"

"Tuna Surprise."

Jane groaned. "What's the surprise — food poisoning?"

"It's not so bad," Toby said. "I can get it down."

"Of course you can. When you've been raised on beef jerky and beans, you can get anything down," Jane joked. "But Andy's used to some of the best cooking in Chicago, and I — well you know the kinds of meals we have at home."

Toby nodded, remembering the artichoke she hadn't known how to eat and the finger bowl water she'd spooned up like soup. "Now that was a surprise all right," she said. "But I'm going to eat dinner anyhow. If I don't eat, I get cranky."

"And if I don't make it into that dance class next year," Andy said, "*I'll* get cranky." The dance department had announced a new advanced dance class, and ever since Andy had heard about it, she'd spent most of her free time working on her audition for it.

"How is it going?" Jane asked.

Andy shook her head. "All right, I guess. But it still needs a lot of work. If I just didn't have to study for finals, too, it wouldn't matter." Suddenly, she laughed. "Listen to me! If I don't study for finals and I flunk, then nothing will matter!"

"True," Jane agreed, taking one more piece of caramel corn and going back to her desk. "I guess it's back to the books."

"Me, too." Toby flopped on to her bed and picked up her geometry book.

Andy stared around the darkened room. It wasn't very cheerful, but it did sort of shut everything out. "I guess I'll give it a try," she said, taking a spiral pad out of her canvas bag. In just a few minutes, she was studying as hard as her roommates, even though she never would understand why a professional ballet dancer — which is what she was determined to be one day — would ever need to know the anatomy of a frog.

But the hushed studying lasted only for about an hour. After that, Andy's mind began wandering to her dance audition. She had some great moves, but there was no theme, nothing to hold those fantastic moves together.

Jane's mind wandered to Cary Slade, her boyfriend who went to Oakley Prep, a boys' school down the road from Canby Hall. She wondered what he was doing now — working at the diner, studying, practicing his guitar? Maybe she'd call him and see if he was in his room. They could talk for a while, and then she could go back to her books. It would be a nice break.

Toby kept thinking of her horse, Max. He was no spring chicken, and her father had mentioned in his last letter that Max had a cough. That was it. "Max has a cough. Don't worry, he's strong as a bull."

Toby sighed. Since her mother had died a

few years before, it had been just she and her
father on the big ranch together. Things had
worked out fine, except that her father was
not a man of many words, and it showed in
his letters. Don't worry about Max? Max was
her working partner on the ranch, her com-
panion, her best animal friend, how could she
not worry about him? Maybe she should call
home, she thought.

All three roommates were trying very hard
not to be the first to quit studying when someone knocked at the door.

"Finally!" Andy said, tossing her notebook
aside and going to the door. "I don't think
I could have kept going a minute longer!"

In the doorway stood their housemother,
Meredith Pembroke, a tall, thin young woman
with dark hair and a confused look on her
face. "What is this?" she asked. "The Gloom
Room?"

"It sure feels like it," Andy agreed. "Actually, we were studying. But come on in, we
can use a break."

Meredith stepped inside and immediately
sniffed the air. "Don't tell me," she said. "Let
me guess. It's definitely something sweet. Not
fudge, though." She took another deep
breath. "It's not cookies, either. I'll tell you
what — if I guess it, I can have some."

"Deal," Andy said.

"I never knew you had such a sensitive nose,
Merry," Jane commented.

"Well, I'm full of surprises." Merry

grinned. "I've got it!" Merry said. "Caramel corn, right?"

"Right you are, that's ten points and a handful of delicious, delectable, Chicago-made caramel corn!" Andy cried, imitating a game show host. Laughing, she flipped on the overhead light and held out the box.

"Delicious is right." Merry chewed for a minute, obviously enjoying it. "Well," she said, swallowing, "now for the real reason I'm here. Ms. Allardyce wants to see you."

A look of panic flitted across the faces of the three roommates. Patrice Allardyce (nicknamed P.A. by the students) was the headmistress of Canby Hall. She was tall, blonde, elegant, and as cool as a cucumber. She'd proved many times that she was a fair headmistress, but she never lost her aloofness, and most of the students went out of *their* way to stay out of *her* way.

Toby asked the question they were all thinking. "What'd we do wrong?"

Meredith laughed. "Who says you did something wrong?"

"P.A. never asks to see students unless they're in trouble," Andy told her.

"Come on, you're exaggerating," Meredith said. "If I knew what she wanted I'd tell you, but she didn't say. She just asked me to send the group from 407 over half an hour before dinner." She checked her watch. "You've got five minutes." Grinning, she left the room.

Toby and Andy were silent, trying to remember if they'd committed any crimes during the week, but Jane stood up briskly. "All right," she said, changing her wrinkled blouse for a crisp blue one that matched her eyes. "We can't show her we're nervous. After all, we don't have anything to be nervous about. Our collective conscience is clear. We have to present a united, guilt-free front."

"Is that a line from the Barrett Family Guide to Battle?" Andy asked.

Jane shook her head. "I just made it up," she said, and then she smiled. "Look at it this way — we wanted an excuse to stop studying, and now we've got it. Let's march!"

"Right, captain!" Andy fell in line behind Jane.

"I'll ride shotgun," Toby said. She scooted next to Jane, and together the three roommates marched out of Baker House.

CHAPTER TWO

"I t looks peaceful enough," Andy commented
when the three of them had reached Ms.
Allardyce's house. The headmistress lived in
a large, white Victorian house with a wrap-
around porch, and it did look peaceful. An
old-fashioned porch swing rocked slightly in
the late afternoon breeze, and even from the
sidewalk, the girls could smell the rich scent
from the lilac bushes that bordered the front
steps.

"Looks can be deceiving, though," Andy
went on. "I wish we'd stopped at the pond
and thrown a penny in for good luck."

"I wish I'd changed my clothes," Toby said,
looking down at her much-washed jeans. "I
don't think Ms. Allardyce likes the way I
dress. And if she's mad already, these old
jeans'll make her madder."

"Nonsense," said Jane, in her crispest, most
upper-class Bostonian style. "You look like

you've been holed up in your room studying. She can't get mad about that." Firmly, she pushed the doorbell. "Remember," she said softly, "our consciences are clear."

When Patrice Allardyce opened her front door, the three girls were standing straight as sticks, their faces as calm and composed as statues. "Meredith gave us your message," Jane said. "You wanted to see us?"

"Yes, I did. Come in, please." Ms. Allardyce pushed open the screen door and led them to her study, where they lined up in front of her desk, their faces like stone.

"Goodness, you three look like soldiers at a court martial," the headmistress commented as she sat in her desk chair. Then her eyebrows shot up, and she gave them a genuine smile. "Relax, please. This is a friendly meeting. In fact, I think you'll be quite flattered once you learn why I've called you here."

Slowly, as if they couldn't quite believe that Ms. Allardyce wasn't going to chew them out about something, Toby, Jane, and Andy sat down on the blue velvet couch. For a moment, everyone smiled at everyone else. Then Toby got restless. "Is it okay to ask what this friendly meeting is about?"

"Of course." Ms. Allardyce cleared her throat, which everyone knew meant she had something important to say. "You remember the week you hosted students interested in attending Canby Hall?"

The girls nodded.

"Well, I just received a letter," the headmistress went on, holding up a sheet of paper, "and it appears that there is one more prospective student who wants to visit our campus. Ordinarily, of course, it would be too late, since the admission committee has already sent out acceptance letters. But this case is very special." She paused, laid the letter down, and smiled at the girls sitting across from her. "And because you three performed so well as hostesses before, I've chosen you to represent our school again and welcome this girl to Canby Hall."

If Ms. Allardyce was expecting enthusiastic smiles of agreement, she didn't get them. All three roommates smiled, of course — it was obviously the thing to do — but they were just being polite. Inside, they were groaning. Play hostess? Now? With finals coming up, it was absolutely the worst possible time to drag some nervous, wide-eyed girl around campus.

The headmistress must have been a mind-reader. "I realize, of course," she said, "that your study load is quite heavy right now, but I'm confident that you can handle both tasks. That's why I chose you."

More polite smiles from the roommates.

Who is this girl, anyway? Andy wondered. Why didn't she take the tour at the regular time with all the others? She must really be a special case, all right. P.A. doesn't bend the rules for just anybody.

Jane was wondering how she was ever

going to explain this to Cary. Both of them were studying hard now, so they couldn't spend much time together. And the time they did spend together was like a treat, like getting dessert after eating all your vegetables. If she had to help show some girl the virtues of Canby Hall, she'd probably have to cut out dessert. And for whom, she wondered? Who is this girl, and why is she so special?

Toby, who was getting restless again, finally asked the question. "Ms. Allardyce, since we're going to be the welcoming committee, could you tell us who we'll be welcoming?"

"Certainly." Ms. Allardyce's eyes sparkled, and her cheeks, usually pale, had two spots of red on them. She was actually excited. "You'll be welcoming Her Royal Highness, the Princess Allegra of Montavia."

"Montavia?" Toby muttered, as the three roommates left the headmistress's house. "Where is that? *What* is that?"

"It's a small country in Europe," Jane said. "About the size of Monte Carlo but not as flashy. It's famous for its skiing, its lakes, and its international banking."

Andy looked at her in amazement. "Where on earth did you learn that?"

"Studying," Jane said. "In a dark room in the middle of a bright spring afternoon." She took a deep breath. "Oh, it's so good to be outside, I can't face going back to the dorm yet. And I definitely can't face Tuna Surprise. Let's go to Pizza Pete's, okay?"

"You're on!" Andy agreed, and the three of them set off for the best (and only) pizza place in Greenleaf.

The minute they entered Pizza Pete's, they realized that not many girls were ready to face Tuna Surprise for dinner. The place was packed. There wasn't an empty booth in sight, and they were reluctantly turning to go when Maggie Morrison spotted them and waved them over.

"We can make room," Maggie said, scooting closer to her roommate, Dee Adams. Maggie was thin, freckled, and bespectacled, and she was one of the warmest, friendliest girls on campus. "Come on, Toby, plant your weary bones right here."

Toby sat down gratefully, while Jane and Andy edged in next to Penny Vanderark, another girl from Baker House.

"Okay, tell us," Dee said immediately. She pushed back her long, California sun-bleached hair and leaned her elbows on the table. "We know P.A. called you over to her house. What did she want? Are you guys in trouble?" Dee always came right to the point.

"Not at all," Jane said. "As a matter of fact, Ms. Allardyce paid us a compliment."

"Some compliment!" Andy hooted. "Showing Princess Allergy around when we're supposed to be studying."

"Allegra," Jane corrected her. "And it *is* a compliment."

"I'm lost," Maggie said. "Why don't you start at the beginning?"

Quickly, Jane told them about the assignment Ms. Allardyce had given them. "Isn't it exciting?" she said. "I can't wait to write Mother and Father about it. They'll be very impressed."

"Well, it takes more than a title to impress me," Andy said, reaching for a slice of hot, cheesy pizza. "Compliment or not, princess or little match girl, this whole thing is a pain in the neck. I've got tons of stuff to do!"

"We all have tons of stuff to do," Jane told her. "But there are three of us, remember? We can share the hostessing. Two days apiece; how does that sound?"

"The princess is going to be here that long?" Penny asked.

"A week," Toby said glumly, wondering what on earth she'd do with a princess.

"She's making a tour of four or five schools in the U.S.," Jane explained. "Canby Hall is her last stop. Wouldn't it be wonderful if she decided to come here?"

"What would be so wonderful about it?" Dee asked bluntly.

"Because Canby Hall's reputation would go up about ten notches," Jane said, as if it should be obvious. "Royalty doesn't send its children to just any old school, you know.

They want the best. We should be proud that she's even considering us."

"Well, it is kind of exciting, I guess," Toby admitted. "The problem is, I'm not exactly used to dealing with princesses. The closest thing we've got to royalty back home is a cattle rancher who owns practically half the county, and he's just a regular guy."

"So maybe this Princess Allegra is just a regular girl," Penny said.

Andy raised her eyebrows. "Somehow, I don't think anybody who's called 'Her Royal Highness' is going to turn out to be a regular girl."

"Speaking of special people," Maggie said with a grin, "I see a very special guy coming this way."

Following her gaze, the others looked and saw Cary Slade threading his way through the crowded restaurant. As Jane raised her hand and waved to him, she thought again how strange it was that he, of all people, was her boyfriend. Both of them were from wealthy, blue blood Boston families, but the similarity stopped there.

While Jane was proud of her Barrett ancestry and her family's standing in the community, Cary wanted nothing to do with his. Not that he hated his family, he just wasn't interested in what "society" was up to.

Jane was extremely preppy; she wore pleated skirts, knee socks, and blazers, all in tasteful, understated colors. Cary, with an earring in one ear, dark glasses, and a wardrobe consisting mainly of jeans, T-shirts, and vests, looked like he belonged with a rock band. He *did* belong to one, in fact; he was the lead guitarist in "Ambulance," a group from Oakley Prep.

Cary loved rock music. Jane's favorite composer was Mozart. Jane was quiet, reserved, and very proper. Cary was easy-going, outgoing, and never did anything by the book.

The two of them were crazy about each other.

"Good evening, everyone," Cary said with a grin. "I stopped over at Baker House, but once I got a whiff of that delectable meal they were serving, I had a feeling that I'd find most of the dorm here."

Jane smiled at him. "Do you want some pizza?"

"Thanks, but I'll catch something at the Greaf." The Greaf Diner (it was originally Greenleaf, but the sign had been missing four letters for so long, nobody called it by its real name) was another favorite eating place in town. Cary had a part-time job there as a counterman. "I've got exactly twenty minutes before I have to get to work," he told Jane, "and I wondered if I could possibly persuade you to take a little stroll through the lovely streets of Greenleaf with me."

As Jane slid out of the booth, Andy laughed. "You sound like a British Lord or something," she said to Cary. "Hey, you wouldn't be interested in escorting a princess around town, would you?"

"Very funny," Jane said, and told Cary all about Princess Allegra.

"Sounds like fun." Cary's blue eyes sparkled. "Allegra," he said softly. "It's a beautiful name. Maybe I'll write a song." He snapped his fingers excitedly. "Yeah, I'll write a song, Ambulance can perform it, and you can bring her ladyship to hear it! Once she knows what kind of talent there is around here, she'll have to choose Canby Hall."

"Um," Jane said uncomfortably. The last thing on earth a princess needed to hear was Ambulance, she thought. But she couldn't tell Cary that. "We, uh, we haven't worked out all our plans yet, but we'll keep it in mind." She took his hand. "Come on, that twenty-minute stroll is already down to fifteen minutes."

But Cary knew what she was thinking, as usual. As they left Pizza Pete's, he laughed. "You should have seen the look on your face when I talked about Ambulance playing for the princess," he teased. "It was like you'd just bitten into a lemon."

"I'm just not sure that a rock band is the right kind of entertainment," Jane said, trying to sound cool.

But Cary wasn't insulted at all. "Don't worry," he said, still laughing. "Royalty isn't my style, so I'll make myself scarce while she's here. The only problem," he went on, putting his arm around her shoulder, "is that while she's here, you're going to be scarce, too."

Jane smiled and slipped her arm around his waist. "It won't be so bad. Andy and Toby have to take a turn with her. Plus, I figured out a way for us to spend a lot of time together, at least for a day or two."

"How?"

"There are two empty rooms in Baker House," Jane told him. "One up on the fifth floor next to Merry's room, and the other in the basement. They're both being used for storage right now. But Ms. Allardyce told us that the rooms have to be painted and decorated — the one upstairs for the princess and the other one for her bodyguards. And she put Andy and Toby and me in charge. So if you volunteer to do a little painting, we'll see more of each other than we would if she weren't coming."

"You supply the paint, and I'll be there," Cary said immediately. He kissed her quickly and hurried into the diner, waving at her through the window as he took his place behind the counter.

Walking back to campus, Jane spotted Toby and Andy just leaving the pizza place and hurried to catch up with them. As they waited for her, Andy said, "Jane's really excited about this princess business."

"Umm," Toby agreed. "I'm sure not. I don't know how to act in front of a royal highness. Will I have to curtsy?"

Andy couldn't help giggling at the thought of Toby curtsying in her stove-pipe jeans. "I don't know," she said. "Jane probably knows. I think she thinks she knows everything about royalty."

"She probably does."

"You're right," Andy admitted. "This kind of thing is right up her alley. She's going to love every minute of it, and that makes us real lucky."

Toby looked doubtful. "How?"

"Well, with Jane in charge," Andy explained, her dark eyes twinkling, "everybody else sort of fades into the background."

"Right," Toby said, catching on. "Which means we might not have to spend very much time with the princess at all."

"You got it," Andy laughed. "Of course, we can't back out unless Jane wants us to."

"No, that wouldn't be fair," Toby agreed.

"But there's nothing wrong with keeping your fingers crossed that she *does* want us to."

"Nothing wrong with that at all," Toby said, and both girls smiled happily as their roommate joined them.

CHAPTER THREE

For the next two days, Baker House was in an uproar. The room that the bodyguards would use had broken cement for a floor, so carpenters were hired to put down a wooden one, and their pounding could be heard in almost every corner of the dorm. Then came the paint crew, which consisted of Cary, Matt — another Oakley Prep student who was Andy's boyfriend — and several girls from Baker House. The pounding was replaced by paint fumes, which drifted down from the attic and up from the basement, meeting somewhere in the middle and causing the residents to open their windows wider than ever. Jane scoured the dorm, interrupting girls in mid-study to ask for donations of plants, lamps, and the softest, fluffiest towels they had.

Amazingly, nobody minded. It was an un-expected break in the middle of the grind of studying, and almost everybody was excited about the idea of a princess coming to visit.

"Do you think she knows Princess Diana?" Maggie asked as she pried open a can of paint.

"I'm sure she does," Jane said. "All the royal families know each other."

"Good," Penny said eagerly. "Maybe she can tell us all kinds of inside information."

"Right," Cary agreed, dipping his roller into a paint pan. "What brand of makeup does Di use? Does Charles ever get holes in his socks? Are Fergie and Andy *really* happy?"

He sounded like a supermarket tabloid, and even Jane had to laugh. "I don't want to spoil things, but I think the royal families have this unspoken agreement not to go around gossiping about each other," she said.

"You're probably right," Maggie agreed. "It won't hurt to ask, though. . . . Just kidding, Jane," she said, laughing at Jane's look of horror.

"I hope so," Jane said. She felt almost totally responsible for making the princess's visit a success. Of course, Andy and Toby were helping, but she could tell their hearts weren't really in it. When Jane had suggested that they paint the princess's room a delicate eggshell white, she'd expected Andy to insist on painting a wild multi-colored mural on one wall, to give it some zing. But Andy had merely nodded, saying that eggshell white sounded good, it went with everything.

And Toby kept fretting about not being

able to curtsy and not being able to carry on a decent conversation with "regular" people, let alone a princess.

Jane understood. They had a lot on their minds. Andy had loads of studying to do, plus she was determined to get into that dance class. Toby needed to study, too, and there was something else worrying her. Jane didn't know what it was. She meant to ask, but she kept putting it off. Whatever it was, it was making Toby quieter and less talkative than usual.

So all that left Jane feeling responsible. She didn't mind, though. And it was funny, she thought. She knew she wasn't the neatest person on earth — after all, her family had a maid and she was used to having her clothes picked up and put away for her. But even though she was a bit of a slob, as Andy would put it, she wasn't sloppy when it came to important things. The more work she had to do, the better organized she was. In the last day and a half, she'd gotten more studying done than she had in a week. And she'd seen more of Cary. That was the best part, she thought as she watched him climb nimbly up a ladder with his paint roller.

"It's looking good, Jane," he said, catching her eye and giving her a wink. "Looks like we'll finish in time."

Jane smiled back, feeling very satisfied. If Princess Allegra chose Canby Hall, it would be a feather in the school's cap, and Jane was going to do everything she could to help put it there.

On the other side of the room, Matt and Andy were using single-edged razor blades to scrape dried paint off the small window.

"This is nice," Matt said. "I didn't think I'd get to see much of you before finals week, so I don't even mind working like a dog as long as you're around."

"Well I don't mind working like a dog, either," Andy told him. "It's just that this isn't the kind of work I had in mind." She sighed and then shook her head, disgusted with herself. "Listen to me. I sound like I'm not even glad to be with you. And I am. It's just that I hate scraping this stupid window when I should be studying."

"Or working on your dance routine?"

Andy nodded. "That's really on my mind," she said. "It's got to be dynamite, or I'll never make the class."

Matt smiled at her. He worked the lights on Canby Hall's dance and theater productions, and he knew all about Andy's dream of becoming a ballerina. He was also her biggest fan.

"Listen," he said. "I know I'm not a choreographer or anything, but I learn a lot up there behind the spotlights. I'd be glad to meet you at the theater sometimes and watch your routine. Who knows? Maybe I could help."

"You promise to be absolutely honest?"

Andy said. "If you hate what I'm doing, you'll tell me? You won't be nice just because you like me?"

"Word of honor," Matt said. "I'll be as critical as they come." He cleared his throat. "Ms. Cord," he said, sounding bored and disgusted, "that is not the kind of dancing that will get you into Advanced Dance. Your technique is laughable, your stage presence is nonexistent. You do have a nice leotard, though. Don't call us, we'll call you." He grinned. "How's that?"

"That," Andy said with a laugh, "is exactly what I'm afraid will happen."

"Come on, you know better."

Andy nodded. "Okay. Let me work on the routine for a day or two more, and then we can meet at the theater and you can pick it apart, step by step." She smiled at him. "Thanks, Matt."

"My pleasure."

Andy picked up her razor blade and started scraping. "I feel better already," she said. "Now if we could just get some food in here, I'd feel great."

"Did I hear somebody say 'food'?" Toby looked up from the baseboard she was painting. "I could use a little something in my stomach. How about if I go get some pizza?"

Everyone agreed that they were ravenous, and after searching through their pockets, they managed to come up with enough for two large pies. In a few minutes, Toby was out of the dorm, striding quickly across the green grass of the campus, and gulping in the fresh air as if she'd spent the last year in a dungeon.

There was nothing wrong with painting a room, of course. Toby could slap paint on a wall with the best of them. And it did make a nice break from her books. It should have been fun, though, but with Max's cough on her mind, she couldn't enjoy all the joking and laughter.

If only there was somebody to talk to about it, she thought. Andy and Jane would have been sympathetic, but she had a hunch they didn't completely understand how much Max meant to her. Besides, they were both so involved in other things right now — Andy in her dance routine, and Jane in her plans for the princess — that they'd probably put a horse's cough way down at the bottom of their list of worries.

The night before, Toby had tried calling her father to find out what was going on. But the phone had rung and rung until she remembered that it was a Friday. And Fridays meant the local ranchers' meeting. Rain or shine, her father never missed one.

By the time she reached town, she was trying to decide whether to call him again tonight or to sit tight and wait until she heard from him, when a horn honked behind her. It was a familiar horn, and as she turned and saw Randy Crowell in his battered pick-up truck, she realized that he was the perfect person to talk to.

"Hey, there!" Randy leaned his blond head out the window and smiled. "Need a lift?"

"I sure do." Toby climbed into the truck and slammed the door. "I'm heading for Pizza Pete's," she said. "But if you're not in any big rush, maybe I could talk to you a minute."

Randy shifted gears and pulled slowly down the street. "Talk away," he said. "I just drove in to get a few supplies — nothing urgent at all."

Randy Crowell was twenty years old and worked on his family's horse farm just outside Greenleaf. He was tall and lean and tan, and Toby had had a crush on him since the second time she met him. Unfortunately, he treated her like his kid sister. It hurt a lot, at first, knowing that he wasn't interested in her, but lately Toby had been seeing another boy. Cornelius Worthington III. She grinned. It was a good thing he was called Neal, she thought; she'd never be able to explain somebody named Cornelius to her dad.

Neal was Jane's former boyfriend, and even though they'd broken up, they were still great friends. Like Jane, he was from Boston's upper class, and he went to a prep school near there. Nobody had been more surprised than Toby when Neal showed an interest in her, but now that she'd gotten used to him, she found she really liked him. He was proper, like Jane, but he wasn't stuffy. He had a good sense of humor, and he liked the outdoors almost as much as Toby. Plus, he made her feel special.

Still, every time she was with Randy, Toby realized that she hadn't quite let go of him. He was the first boy she'd ever really cared about, and even though she ordered it not to, her stomach did a funny little flip-flop every time she saw him.

Right now, though, her mind wasn't on her stomach. It was on Max. "What would you do if one of your horses started coughing?" she asked. That was another good thing about Randy — he knew his horses.

"What kind of cough?" Randy said.

Toby shrugged. "Dad didn't say."

"You mean it's Max?"

"Mmm. Could it be a cold, do you think? Or pneumonia?" Toby asked.

"Whoa, don't get carried away," Randy said. "What else did your father say about it?"

"Nothing. He's about as wordy as I am," Toby told him. "Well, he did say not to worry, but — "

"Then don't," Randy broke in firmly. "Now horses do catch colds, you know, just like people. But Max isn't some delicate thoroughbred who's used to being coddled. He's probably had plenty of aches and pains over the years and never even mentioned them."

Toby had to smile.

"That's better," Randy said. "Besides, from

what you say, your father knows more about horses than almost anybody. He can handle it, so trust him."

"You're right," Toby agreed. "But it sure is a bother, being so far away."

"Well, it won't be long before you're home," Randy said, pulling up in front of the pizza place. "Got any big plans for the summer?"

"I can't see that far ahead," Toby told him. "I've got to get the final exams out of the way first." Suddenly, she remembered something else she might have to get out of the way — Princess Allegra. "What would you say," she asked Randy, "if I was to bring a real live princess out to your farm to ride?"

Randy laughed. "I'd say, 'pleased to meet you, your highness.'"

"I guess that'll do," Toby said, and told him all about the upcoming royal visit. "Now I might not have to do anything with her," she went on, "because Jane's already got so many plans, it'd take three weeks to get through them. But just in case I do get stuck having to entertain her, I thought I'd better check with you first."

"Bring her on out," Randy said, laughing at the idea of a princess visiting his farm. "I don't think we have a red carpet to roll out, though. Will a horse blanket do?"

"It'll have to," Toby laughed, opening the door and hopping out of the truck. Grinning, she stood on the running board and peered in the window. "Just make sure it doesn't have any fleas — I have a feeling that princesses are mighty particular people!"

Although she wouldn't have used Toby's words, Jane also had a feeling that princesses were mighty particular. And as she inspected the finished fifth-floor room on Sunday morning, she tried to look at it as critically as possible.

On the floor was a remnant of beige carpet that Meredith had unearthed in the storeroom. Fortunately, the room wasn't big, so the remnant went from wall to wall and the unfinished edges didn't show. Neither did the stain, which had been strategically placed under the bed.

The bed was a regular Canby Hall single, but Jane had put some of her own crisp white sheets on it, and borrowed a fluffy, down-filled comforter in a dusty rose color. The weather was too warm for down, of course, but the comforter was too luxurious to pass up.

A desk and a chest of drawers, painted the same eggshell as the room, stood against one wall. And against another, Jane had put a white wicker chair with a cushion the same color as the comforter. A beautiful green plant hung in front of the window, and another stood in a basket in one corner. Ms. Allardyce had contributed the plants, as well as the vase of white and purple lilacs that sat on the desk.

It was fine, Jane thought. She picked a piece of lint off the carpet and looked around again. It was better than fine. It was a room fit for a princess.

Suddenly, Jane heard somebody shout, "She's here!" Giving the room one final glance, she closed the door and went downstairs to help welcome Princess Allegra to Canby Hall.

CHAPTER FOUR

At ten-thirty on Sunday morning, every girl in Baker House was hanging her head out a window. Some had just come out of the shower and had towels wrapped around their heads; others had interrupted their studies and were blinking like owls in the bright sun. Girls coming back from church, tennis, and breakfast in town gathered on the lawn or in the main hall, waiting. Nobody wanted to miss the first glimpse of Princess Allegra.

The stately black limousine drove slowly down the drive and pulled to a majestic stop in front of the entrance to the dorm. Ms. Allardyce stood alone at the bottom of the steps, and behind her, gathered near the door, were Meredith, Andy, Jane, and Toby. Toby tried to smooth a wrinkle out of her denim skirt and then gave up. She glanced around at the large group of girls, her green eyes slightly panicked, as if she were trying to spot an escape route.

"Stop fidgeting," Jane whispered.

"Sorry." Toby tried to stand still. "Crowds always make me want to run like a jackrabbit. Do you suppose the princess feels that way?"

Jane shook her head. "I'm sure she's used to being stared at."

"Let's hope so," Andy said. "When she gets out of that classy limo, there's going to be at least two hundred eyes, all looking straight at her."

The driver got out then and opened one of the back doors. Everyone grew quiet, expecting the princess, but instead, two men in dark suits emerged.

"Footmen?" Andy quipped.

"No, security," Jane said. "You know — bodyguards."

The two men were both tall, muscular, and unsmiling, and their eyes darted suspiciously over the group of students.

"What are they looking for?" Andy said. "A poisoned Bic pen?"

Toby couldn't help laughing, which earned her a frown from Ms. Allardyce.

"Ssh!" Jane hissed. "She's getting out now!"

The chattering and whispering stopped, and all eyes (two hundred of them, according to Andy) focused on the slender girl who was climbing gracefully out of the limousine. She wore a softly pleated, lemon-yellow dress and a linen blazer the color of coffee with extra cream. The sun picked out the auburn in her dark hair, which tumbled to her shoulders in loose, wavy curls, and her eyes, even from a distance, looked as big as saucers.

She's beautiful, Jane thought.

Toby thought, there aren't any like her back in Texas, that's for sure.

She looks like a princess, Andy thought, and then smiled to herself. She is a princess, you idiot.

With a lovely smile, Princess Allegra walked to the steps of Baker House and shook hands with Patrice Allardyce. Toby sighed in relief. At least there wasn't going to be any curtsying.

The headmistress, very elegant herself in a beige suit and white silk blouse, looked as if greeting royalty was something she did every day of her life. "Princess Allegra," Ms. Allardyce said, "on behalf of everyone here at Canby Hall, let me welcome you to our school. We're very pleased to have you here, and we hope your visit will be both informative and enjoyable."

The princess nodded, smiled, and spoke softly.

"What'd she say?" Andy whispered.

"She said, 'thank you,'" Jane told them, barely moving her lips. "What did you expect her to say?"

"As you can see," the headmistress went on, "your visit has created a lot of excitement." She gestured toward the open windows of

Baker House and frowned as several girls waved enthusiastically. "But, according to your wishes, we've tried to do everything to make certain that you feel like just another resident in the dorm. You have your own room, of course, but that can't be helped, since no others were available, and you do need special arrangements for your security personnel."

The princess nodded, and looking up at the windows of Baker House, she smiled shyly.

"Aside from that," Ms. Allardyce said, "you'll be taking your meals with everyone else . . ."

"Wait'll she tastes the meatloaf," Andy muttered.

". . . and you'll share the showers . . ."

"Uh-oh," Toby whispered. "I hope she likes 'em cold."

" . . . and you'll be expected to abide by all the rules of the dormitory, including the nightly curfew."

"You hear that?" Meredith whispered to the residents of 407. "Just don't show her any of the tricky ways to sneak back in after hours."

"What tricky ways?" Andy asked innocently.

"And now, let me introduce you to your housemother, Meredith Pembroke," Ms. Allardyce said. "If you have any questions or problems, Ms. Pembroke is the one to whom you speak."

Meredith and the princess shook hands, and then Ms. Allardyce turned to the three roommates. "And these are the girls I've chosen to be your guides during you stay here at Canby Hall. Jane Barrett, Andrea Cord, and October Houston."

One by one, the princess shook their hands, telling each that she was glad to meet them. When she got to Toby, she said, "October. What a lovely name. Is it a family one?"

"Uh, no." Toby felt uncomfortable being singled out. "I was born in the month of October. That's where it came from. Most folks call me Toby."

"Shall I?" the princess asked.

"Uh, sure." Toby bobbed her head like a puppet. "That'll be fine."

"Now, your hostesses will show you to your room," Ms. Allardyce said, "and then you can begin your day." Looking at the crowd of spectators, she raised her eyebrows. The girls took the hint, ducking back into their windows or wandering away from the dorm. The driver of the limousine started unloading luggage, and flanked by her bodyguards, Princess Allegra of Montavia entered Baker House.

Half an hour later, Maggie Morrison stuck her head around the door of Room 407 and looked expectantly at Toby and Andy. "Well? What's she like? What did she think of her room? Did you see any of the clothes she brought?"

Andy, wearing a bright orange leotard and

yellow legwarmers, stopped in the middle of a kneebend and grinned. "Who?" she asked teasingly.

"Princess Allegra, as if you didn't know," Maggie laughed. "Come on, tell me all about her."

Dee's blonde head appeared in the doorway behind Maggie. "My roommate has developed a raging case of royalty worship," she said. "In fact, I think the entire dorm has come down with it. It's an epidemic. I'm going to get out of here before I catch it." With a quick wave, she strode down the hall.

Maggie laughed again. "Dee's as curious as everybody else," she said. "She just won't admit it. You wait, tonight she'll pump me for information."

"Well, Jane's taking her on her first tour right now, so we can't really tell you much," Andy said. She stretched one leg out on her desk and touched her head to her knee. "Toby? What's the princess like?"

"Huh?" Toby was working on a letter to her father, asking him about Max. They wrote once a month, and she hoped if he got a letter from her when he wasn't expecting it, he'd answer right back. "Oh, the princess. She was kind of quiet. I figured she was tired."

"Did she say anything about the room?"

Andy stretched her other leg out. "She said it was charming. Then she asked to see 407, so she'd know what kind of room she'd have if she decided to come here."

"I thought Jane was going to fall through the floor when the princess said that." Toby laughed and pointed toward Jane's bed, which was almost buried under a pile of discarded clothes and spiral notebooks. "But she did some real fast talking and managed to put it off."

"But you're not telling me anything about the princess," Maggie protested.

Andy stopped stretching and reached for a wrap-around skirt that matched her leotard. "Like I said, there's not much to tell yet. We're splitting our hostessing duties, and it's not my turn yet. It's a good thing, too," she said, snatching up a canvas bag and heading for the door, "because this is one girl who's got more to do than be an ambassador for Canby Hall. I've got a dance routine to work out, and if I don't get it right pretty soon, I might as well kiss that dance class good-bye." In a flash of orange, she was gone.

Maggie sighed. "Well, if I want to learn anything about the princess, I guess I'll just have to wait till Jane gets back. You and Andy don't seem interested at all."

"I think we'd be more interested if we didn't have to have anything to do with her," Toby admitted. "Andy's all skittish about that dance class, and you know me — I get tongue-tied just thinking about being with somebody I don't know." She chewed her pencil for a second and then grinned. "But you're right about Jane — she'll be the one to talk to. I bet she's happier than a cow in clover right now."

Toby was wrong. Instead of feeling like a cow in clover, Jane was beginning to feel more like a fish out of water. And she couldn't quite put her finger on why.

Things had started out fine. Princess Allegra had been very impressed with the room, and Jane was secretly flattered. She'd suggested that they take a stroll around the campus before lunch, and the princess seemed to think that was a good idea. She'd changed quickly into a pair of yellow sandals, white cotton pants, and a blue silk blouse with the sleeves rolled up above her elbows. If anything, the outfit was even more elegant than the one in which she'd arrived. And with the two security men following them at a discreet distance, there was no way the princess could blend in with the rest of the girls on campus.

Jane had showed the princess the Main Building, pointing out the portrait of Julia Canby, who had died young and whose father had founded the school in her name. She'd shown her Barrett Hall, and Allegra commented on the name. "Yes," Jane said, pleased that she'd noticed. "My grandfather gave the building to the school." She started to explain about the long association between Canby Hall and the Barretts of Boston, but stopped herself. It might sound a bit snobbish.

After a quick look at the library, the

auditorium, and the other dorms —Charles and Addison Houses — they strolled around the grounds again. Jane pointed out Ms. Allardyce's home, the skating pond and playing fields, and finally, they stopped at the wishing pond.

"It's a tradition," Jane said as they looked down at the pennies glittering on the mossy bottom of the pool. "Girls make wishes about everything, but mostly about boys and grades."

"I see," the princess said. "I suppose there are a lot of traditions in a school like Canby Hall."

"Oh, yes," Jane agreed. "There's the spring carnival, and the autumn leaf-rake. Everyone hates the leaf-rake, but I think if it were canceled, people would actually miss it."

The princess smiled and nodded.

"I think traditions are important," Jane went on enthusiastically, deciding she'd found a subject in which Allegra was interested. "Of course, we gripe about them or make fun of them sometimes, but that's a tradition, too. When it comes down to it, most of us would feel lost without them."

Suddenly, Jane realized she'd been hogging the conversation, as Toby would say, which was considered bad form in Boston as well as in Texas. She stopped and waited, so the princess could have a chance to say something.

Silence.

Maybe she doesn't agree with me about

tradition, Jane thought and turned to see if that was the problem.

Princess Allegra was still staring into the wishing pond, her dark eyes fastened firmly on the pennies. Jane would have thought she was fascinated with them, except for one thing — her mouth was open in a wide, jaw-stretching yawn.

Then, as Jane was trying to decide whether to say something sympathetic about how tired the princess must be — not that she looked tired — or to just ignore the yawn, she glanced across the pond and saw Gigi Norton.

Wearing too much makeup as usual, Gigi (dubbed by Jane as The Worst Person in the World), parted her red lips in a sarcastic smile. "Well, Jane," she called across the pond. "I see you've managed to bore the princess already. Ms. Allardyce is going to be very unhappy if she hears about this!"

CHAPTER FIVE

Jane felt her cheeks get hot. If she'd been alone, she would have been tempted to forget her Back Bay upbringing and tell Gigi to join the pennies at the bottom of the pond. But she didn't want to get into a nasty war of words in front of Princess Allegra. Besides, Gigi's comment made her wonder — had she been boring the princess? Jane thought the traditions of Canby Hall were interesting. Surely a princess, who had all kinds of traditions to follow, would have to agree that they were important. Anyway, she was the one who'd brought the subject up.

Jane was flustered, a feeling she wasn't used to and didn't like. If that yawn was a sign of boredom, then Gigi was right — Ms. Allardyce wouldn't be happy.

Inwardly fuming at Gigi's sense of timing, Jane had no choice but to introduce her to Allegra. She just hoped the princess didn't

44

get the idea that Gigi was a typical Canby Hall girl, or she'd catch the next train out of town.

"I couldn't help hearing what you said just now," Princess Allegra said to Gigi after they'd shaken hands. "Jane was being very entertaining, actually, and it was rude of me to have yawned." She laughed lightly. "But I wasn't bored at all. You see, I've been traveling for three weeks, and I'm afraid I'm tired. When you're tired, you sometimes forget your manners. I'm sure you know the feeling."

It was a perfect little speech, Jane thought in admiration. It let her off the hook and put Gigi Norton on it. Gigi struggled for a few seconds but then gave up. "Well," she said, trying to sound casual, "I have to go study. Finals are coming up." With an awkward smile, she turned and left.

To Jane's surprise, the princess burst out laughing. Not the polite, tinkly laugh she'd given before, but a strong one that came straight from the stomach. "That was fun!" she said, turning to Jane with a gleam in her eyes. "I didn't like what she said to you, so I wanted to take her down a peg. I must admit, I enjoyed it, but I hope I didn't hurt her feelings too badly."

"Don't worry about it too much," Jane told her. "Gigi's skin is as thick as an alligator's."

"Good." The princess laughed again, and then said, "I do apologize for that yawn, you know. But what I said was true — I'm tired. And hungry! Isn't it about time for lunch?"

"Half an hour," Jane said. "But I thought we might have lunch in town. There's a nice place — the Greenleaf Inn — that serves great club sandwiches. Almost nobody from Canby Hall goes there, except on special occasions. So it'll be nice and peaceful."

Jane was looking forward to a quiet lunch at the Inn, where they had white linen tablecloths and real sprigs of mint in the iced tea. She fully expected the princess to feel the same way. Then she saw that Princess Allegra's face had lost its sparkle.

"There's no rule about eating lunch at the dining hall," Jane said quickly, thinking that might be the problem.

"I almost wish there were," the princess said. "Then it would be fun to eat at the Greenleaf Inn."

"I don't understand," Jane told her.

Princess Allegra sighed and shook her head. "Jane, you're being a perfectly lovely hostess, so please don't be insulted by what I'm about to say."

Totally confused, Jane nodded.

"You see," Princess Allegra said, "I've toured three other schools in the past three weeks, and in each one, my guides treated me like I'm made out of spun glass. I understand of course, and I don't blame them. After all, it's the way I've been treated my whole life — it's as though I've been living in a cocoon for seventeen years." She sighed again. "But I'm going to be honest, Jane. I'm tired, yes. But mostly I'm tired of being so sheltered, of being treated so properly and carefully." She spun around, spreading her arms wide. "I want to be treated like a normal person, can you understand that? I want to trade insults with somebody like your Gigi Norton. I want to sneak out of the dorm after hours or have illegal parties in my room or paper the lilac bushes at Ms. Allardyce's house, or whatever you do here at Canby Hall when you feel like being wicked."

Jane, who'd never felt like being wicked in her life, nodded again.

"It's not that I don't appreciate all the history and tradition of a school like Canby Hall," the princess went on. "I do. But I want to experience the other half of life here. The real half."

Jane cleared her throat. "I see," she said. "I think."

Princess Allegra reached out a hand and touched Jane's shoulder. "You're not insulted, are you? I haven't hurt your feelings, I hope, because I'd feel terrible if I had."

"No, no," Jane said. "Not at all."

"Good." Allegra yawned again, and then blushed as her stomach rumbled loudly. "Sorry. I'm famished. Let's go to the dining hall, shall we?"

Together, the two girls, trailed by the security people, strolled back across the campus. Jane, who happened to know that today's lunch was ground ham patties —

otherwise known as pig à la hockey puck — couldn't help smiling to herself. It was going to be interesting to see what the princess thought of her first taste of real life at Canby Hall.

When Andy got back from the auditorium around one o'clock, she turned into Room 407, stopped, and stepped back out to make sure she had the right room. Yep — 407 — there it was, right on the door. Still amazed, she went inside.

Jane's side of the room was sparkling clean. No socks or shirts or notebooks littered the floor. No empty soda cans stuck to the desk and the window ledge. For the first time in months, the antique cross-stitch quilt that covered Jane's bed was actually visible.

Andy heard a thump in the vicinity of the closet and grinned. "Hey!" she called. "What's with the clean-up routine? You must be expecting some real special company!"

Jane backed out of the closet carrying an armload of wadded-up towels. Her cheeks were smudged and her hair was a mass of tangles. "I want you to know," she said, "that I gave up an hour's worth of studying to get this place in order. When I flunk the history test, I'll be able to come back and cry in a clean room."

Andy laughed. "I take it the princess is going to pay a visit to 407."

Jane nodded. "In about half an hour," she

said. "I thought I was done, but I just found these towels in a corner of the closet. What do you think — are they worth saving?"

"Are you kidding? Those things probably have three generations of germs growing on them by now." Andy held open the green trash bag that was in the center of the room. "Put them in here before we contaminate the place."

Jane tossed in the towels and then surveyed the room. Satisfied that it was more presentable than it had ever been, she reached for her hairbrush. "Andy?" she said casually. "There's something I want to talk to you about."

"Okay, shoot." Andy had peeled off her leotard and was tying a lightweight lavender robe around her waist.

As well as she could, Jane explained what Princess Allegra had said about wanting a normal, real-life experience during her stay at Canby Hall.

"Well, that makes sense," Andy said, taking a fresh towel from her bureau and draping it over her shoulder. "I mean, she'll never learn what this place is all about if she stays in her ivory tower up there on the fifth floor."

"I suppose," Jane said doubtfully. "Anyway, I was thinking. Since you're so real — "

"What do you mean, *I'm* real?!" Andy laughed. "What does that make you and Toby — ghosts?"

"Of course not," Jane replied. "I just meant

that you're the kind of person who could show the princess the side of Canby Hall that she's interested in. I'm not the most spontaneously fun person in the world — you know that. And Toby always takes a long time to warm up to people. . . ."

"I think I see what's coming," Andy said. "You want me to take my turn with her royal highness now, don't you?"

"Please?" Jane asked hopefully. "I promise I'll take another turn before she leaves."

Andy thought about it. As far as she was concerned, the princess should have just been left on her own for part of the time. After all, she was a big girl, she didn't need somebody with her every minute of every day. Nobody else got that kind of treatment.

Besides, Andy had to study. She'd been spending so much time on her dance routine that if she didn't crack a book pretty soon, her grades would go into a tailspin.

Still, she knew it wasn't just Jane's job. She and Toby had been secretly hoping that Jane and the princess would really hit it off so the two of them wouldn't have to spend any time with her. But it looked like things weren't going to work out that way. All right, Andy, she told herself, take your medicine. Then you can pass it on to Toby.

"Okay," she said. "I'll do it. I've got to check some books out of the library and then I'm meeting Matt at the auditorium. But maybe after that, we can go to The Greaf. She can't complain that that's too fancy."

"Thanks, Andy," Jane said gratefully. "You're a *real* friend!"

Laughing, Andy went off to take a quick shower. When she got back, Jane had gone, Toby was still out, and Princess Allegra was sitting in one of the desk chairs, staring up at the tea bag.

"How do you like it?" Andy asked with a grin.

The princess laughed. "I wouldn't bet on it becoming a national craze. Whose is it, and what does it mean?"

"It's Toby's." Andy unwrapped the towel from her head and reached for the blow dryer. Over the whine of the motor, she went on, "She put it up the second day she got here, and still hasn't told anyone why. I could understand if it were a horseshoe, or a picture of stars — she really misses those Texas skies — but a tea bag's a real mystery."

Snapping off the dryer, Andy stepped into a pair of baggy tapered pants and pulled on a bright red, oversized T-shirt. As she dressed, she explained to the princess what the schedule was that afternoon.

Princess Allegra nodded and smiled, but didn't say anything, and Andy decided she was disappointed. What does she want me to do? Andy wondered. Drop everything and organize a party or something? It wasn't fair, she thought. The princess should have enough brains to realize that we're all busy. Suddenly, she began to resent this royal visitor, and even though she was usually so talkative that people had to stand in line to get a word in, she said almost nothing as the two of them walked to the library.

When they left, the princess was surrounded by the other students, who wanted a chance to meet her and talk to her. Andy was forced to stand at the side and wait, her foot tapping impatiently, while Princess Allegra fielded questions about everything from who her favorite rock group was to whether she had a boyfriend. She was friendly and relaxed, and Andy couldn't help admiring the way she managed to answer the personal questions without actually giving anything away.

"I'm sorry about that," the princess said, when the two were finally able to head for the auditorium.

Andy shrugged. "I guess you can't help it."

"Yes, it's too late now," the princess agreed. "But I do wish I'd been able to arrive here without any fanfare at all. Just sort of slip in without anyone knowing who I am. Then I wouldn't feel so much on display."

Suddenly, Andy felt like defending the other girls. "Well, you can't really blame people for paying attention to you. They're just curious. Wouldn't you be if you were in their shoes?"

"I suppose you're right," Princess Allegra

said. "Yes, you're absolutely, right. I was complaining and I shouldn't have. Thank you for pointing that out, Andy."

Way to go, Cord, Andy thought, as they entered the auditorium. Now you've insulted her. Face it — you're not cut out to be a diplomat.

Inside, Andy introduced the princess to Matt, then quickly changed her clothes in one of the dressing rooms. When she came out, she forgot about being a diplomat, and concentrated on being a dancer.

"It's like an Olympic skating routine," she said to Matt. "There are certain moves I have to do, but it's up to me to decide how to work them in." She shook her head. "I still don't understand why we have to choreograph our own routines."

"They probably want to see if you've got any imagination," Matt said. "Why don't you just go through what you've got so far. Then we can talk about it."

Nodding, Andy slipped a cassette into Matt's small tape recorder and took her place in the center of the stage. Matt sat in the front row, Princess Allegra was a few rows behind him, and the two body guards hovered together at the back, but as far as Andy was concerned, they might as well have been in the next county. The minute she started to dance, she forgot everything but the movement of her body as it twirled and swayed and leaped across the stage. When she finished, she held her final pose for a beat, then bent from the waist, breathing hard. "Well?" she asked.

"You've got an imagination, all right," Matt said, bounding onto the stage. "But maybe it's a little overactive."

Andy frowned. "What do you mean?"

"I mean you've got everything in that routine but the kitchen sink. You want to dazzle them, not make them dizzy."

Andy nodded. "I guess I figured if I could do one good leap, why not do five?"

"Three would be plenty," Matt said. "The way it is now, the whole thing just looks too busy. If you cut out a few of the hops, skips, and jumps, it'll all hold together better."

Andy grinned. "Okay, dancemaster, let's get to it."

They worked for another forty-five minutes, until three girls needed the stage to rehearse a scene for their acting final. Matt had to leave anyway — he wanted to get some studying in before dinner — so after saying good-bye, Andy and the princess walked outside.

"I know I should go straight back to Baker House and shower," Andy said, "but I didn't have any lunch. And if I don't get something in my stomach in the next few minutes, I'll collapse."

"I did have lunch," Princess Allegra said. "And the sooner I put something decent in my stomach, the sooner I'll be able to forget what lunch tasted like."

Andy burst out laughing. At least the princess had a sense of humor. "Come on, then," she said. "Let's go fill up before dinner."

When the two of them stepped inside the Greaf, Cary immediately waved them over to the counter. Andy introduced them, and Cary, his eyes twinkling, opened their menus with a flourish. "Thank you for gracing our humble diner with your presence," he said. "It's an honor to serve you."

"Hey, what about me?" Andy asked.

"It's always an honor to serve you, Ms. Cord." Cary whipped out his order pad. "What's your pleasure?"

Both girls ordered cheeseburgers, french fries, and Cokes. Cary nodded. "I'll speak to the varlet in the kitchen at once," he told them. Bowing from the waist, he turned on his heels and left them.

Andy laughed and shook her head. "Cary's a little crazy, but he's one of the nicest guys I've ever met. He's Jane's boyfriend, you know."

Princess Allegra stared at her in amazement.

"I know, it's kind of hard to believe," Andy said. "But they really do hit it off."

"Does he go to school around here, or does he live in Greenleaf?"

"School," Andy told her. She described Oakley Prep. "Matt goes there, too, lucky for me."

"You *are* lucky, to have such a helpful boyfriend," Princess Allegra said. "But I don't expect you'll be needing anybody's help for much longer — not in dance, anyway. You're very talented."

The words were simple, but it was obvious that the princess meant them, and Andy was flattered and pleased. "Thanks," she said. "I have a long way to go, but I think I'll get there."

Suddenly, the kitchen door banged open and Cary reappeared, a metal tray held high over his head. "Fresh off the grill," he announced, "two superbly prepared burgers topped with creamy melted cheese, two orders of exquisitely crisp french fries, and two ice-cold Cokes, guaranteed to quench any thirst." He arranged the plates in front of them and turned to the princess. "Sorry, your Highness, our silver goblets are tarnished from lack of use."

Princess Allegra pretended to be outraged. "I'll have to speak to the manager."

"At your service, mademoiselle." Cary bowed again, his hand at his chest, and then straightened up, grinning from ear to ear.

"You're the manager, too?" she asked.

"When did you get promoted?" Andy wanted to know.

"Since the real manager went to the dentist," Cary told them. "And now, if you'll excuse me, I must attend to some new arrivals." Bowing one last time, he sauntered down to the end of the counter, where the security guards had seated themselves.

"This is wonderful," Princess Allegra said after her first big bite of cheeseburger. "Just think, when I come to the states next year, I'll be able to have one of these every single day if I want to."

"You mean you can't get hamburgers in Montavia?" Andy asked.

"I'm sure you can." Princess Allegra gave a funny little smile. "But not where I live."

"Oh, right. I guess they would seem a little out of place in a palace dining room."

"Mmm." Princess Allegra bit into a french fry and nodded. "Cheese straws are about as daring as they get when it comes to finger food." She smiled again. "If most of the girls who talked to me today found out what my life was really like, they'd be disappointed — it's very structured, very isolated, very unexciting."

As they continued eating, Andy started to get an idea of what the princess meant. She wasn't free to come and go as she chose; she was tutored in the palace; her best friend was a cousin who was in a Swiss boarding school and could only visit twice a year; and she had to attend every royal dinner, banquet, garden party, and speech, no matter how boring. She told all this without complaining and even managed to make some of it sound funny, but Andy could tell she wasn't completely thrilled with her life.

"Now I know what you meant when you told Jane you wanted to experience the 'real' life at Canby Hall," Andy said. "You really do live in an ivory tower."

"Yes, but I'm getting out for a whole year," the princess said excitedly. "I had to fight for it, of course. My parents were both opposed, but when I threatened to break my engagement, they gave in gracefully."

Andy wasn't sure she'd heard right. "You threatened to break your what?"

"My engagement." The princess laughed at the look on Andy's face. "Yes, it's true. I'm engaged to be married to Prince Frederick of Almare. It's a small principality that borders Montavia, but once we're married there's going to be a grand union of the two countries. Our families couldn't be happier."

For once in her life, Andy was speechless.

CHAPTER SIX

Princess Allegra laughed again. "Don't look so shocked. They didn't arrange the marriage when I was two, or anything like that. But we have been sort of groomed for each other for about that long. Frederick is thirty-four. He seems like a decent man, but what do I know about men? What do I know about anything, really?" She finished her last french fry and helped herself to the ones Andy had left over. "That's why I made this bargain with my family — I get to spend a year abroad, on my own. Then I'll go back home and be the best princess I know how to be."

Andy finally found her voice. "You mean you have to get married right after you graduate?"

"That's the plan."

"But what's the rush?"

"Money and politics," the princess announced. "In other words, our marriage is going to help both countries. Besides, what else would I do?"

"Well, there's college, for one thing. Or a job, or travel, or just hanging out." Andy could easily have come up with a dozen things even a princess could do besides get married, but she stopped herself. "Never mind. It's really none of my business."

"That's all right," Princess Allegra said. "I enjoy hearing your ideas." She sipped some Coke and then looked at Andy. "Do you know, that's the first time you've asked me anything about my life? And I was the one who brought it up. Are you really not curious about me or were you just being polite?"

"Oh, I'm as curious as the next person." Andy squirmed a little on the stool. "I guess I didn't want to be like everybody else, treating you like somebody special just because you're a princess."

The princess nodded thoughtfully. "Well, I am special, I think, but not because of my title. Just like you're special. But I'll bet what most people see first is the color of your skin."

"You know, you're right," Andy said, surprised, seeing her suddenly not as a princess, but as a girl named Allegra with whom she might like to be friends. "It's changed now, but when I first came here, I stuck out like a sore thumb, or I thought I did."

"I know the feeling," Allegra told her.

Andy grinned and held out her hand to

shake. "As a former sore thumb to a new one, welcome to Canby Hall."

That night, after no one could absorb a single more fact from a book, there was an impromptu party in Room 407. The three residents and four guests made quick work of Andy's caramel corn, and when Princess Allegra — whose bodyguards thought she was fast asleep — crept up to her room and returned with a basket of fresh fruit and a box of French chocolates, the feast continued.

Toby was preoccupied and didn't say much, but the others had a great time. As the party went on, they started to realize what Andy had discovered earlier — that she was a nice girl with a good sense of humor and a big appetite for fun. She loved to talk and was as interested in them as they were in her. After they went over all their differences — the biggest one being that Allegra was engaged — they found that they had plenty in common. They compared notes on everything from clothes to hair styles to rock groups, and by the time the party was over, everyone felt that she was their friend.

The princess spent her second day at Canby Hall with Andy, who didn't mind at all this time. Nothing exciting happened, but Allegra didn't seem to care what they did as long as it was "normal." Since a normal day at Canby Hall consisted of going to class, studying, talking, and trying to eat the so-called food in the cafeteria, that's what they did. And because of the party the night before, the princess seemed to fit right in. The only abnormal thing she had to do was have tea with Ms. Allardyce, and Jane was about the only person who envied her for that.

While Allegra was with the headmistress, Andy went to the library, and Jane and Toby tried to get some studying done in their room before dinner.

"It's nice that Andy and Allegra get along so well, isn't it?" Jane said after highlighting for a while. "I mean, it's nice for them, naturally, but it's nice for Canby Hall, too. It means the chances of her choosing it are that much better."

Toby, whose head was in her biology book and whose mind was on Max, said, "Mmm."

"Can you believe she's engaged?" Jane went on. "It seems so medieval, doesn't it?"

"Mmm."

Jane looked over at Toby. "Did you know that Baker House is on fire?"

"Mmm."

"I thought so." Jane shut her book with a slap, which made Toby finally look up.

"Did you say something?" Toby asked.

"I said lots of somethings," Jane laughed. "And you didn't hear any of them. I didn't know you were that fascinated with biology."

"I'm not," Toby admitted with a sigh. "I've been staring at the same paragraph for ten minutes, and I don't know what it says."

"Switch subjects for a while," Jane suggested.

"That's not the problem." Toby took a deep breath. "The problem's Max."

"Max?" For a second, Jane couldn't remember who Max was. Then her eye fell on Toby's bedside picture. "Oh, yes, your horse. What did Max do?"

"Coughed," Toby said miserably. "Dad wrote me that he had a cough. I tried to call, but Dad was out, so I wrote him right back, asking him to let me know real quick what was going on. He'll probably get the letter in a couple of days." She took another deep breath. "Max is sick, and I can't think about anything else."

"Don't wait for your father to get that letter," Jane told her. "Call him again."

"I'm afraid to," Toby said. "What if it's bad news?"

Jane had grown up in a household without pets. The closest she'd ever come to feeling the way Toby felt now was about a stray cat she and her older sister Charlotte had hidden and fed in the kitchen for almost a week before being discovered. It didn't matter that the cook found a friendly, animal-loving home to send it to — Jane had missed that cat for months. Of course, she'd never felt it was her intellectual equal, while Toby seemed to think Max was smarter than a lot of people. Still, during the few days it had been her pet, she'd loved it.

"Listen," she said firmly to Toby, "I'm sure your father would call you if anything really awful was happening. He knows how much Max means to you. That horse is probably just fine by now, and your father probably wishes he'd never even mentioned it."

Toby thought about it for a minute, then shook her head. "If it was just a piddly little thing, he wouldn't have said a word. I think he's trying to get me ready for what's down the road."

Jane didn't know Mr. Houston, but from what Toby had said, he wasn't the kind of man to talk about "piddly" little things. Maybe Toby was right. "Then I think you should call him," she said again.

"I told you, I'm scared to. But I can't go on feeling as jumpy as a cat on a griddle," she admitted. "I'll give him three days, and if I don't hear from him, I'll call."

"Good." Jane turned back to her book, Toby went back to hers, and when Andy came in a few minutes later, she found them both studying as if finals started the next day.

"They should take a picture of this for their brochure," she joked. " 'Two Canby Hall girls spend a typical evening studying in their room.' "

"That would be false advertising," Jane pointed out. "Last night was much more typical than this."

"Yeah, that was fun, wasn't it?" Andy

agreed. "Too bad about finals, or we could do it again tonight."

"Let's do it anyway," Jane said. "We can set a half-hour time limit, but at least we'll get another taste of those incredible French chocolates."

Andy grinned at her. "Seems to me I saw the last one disappear down your throat last night," she said.

"I only had two!" Jane protested.

"Two at a time, you mean!"

Jane tossed a pillow at her, which Andy immediately tossed back, and the two of them were just about ready to get into a full-fledged pillow fight when the phone rang. Before either one of them could stop laughing and make a move to get it, Toby had shot up from her bed like a streak, reaching the phone in about two seconds.

"Hello?" she said breathlessly, as if she'd just run twenty yards instead of two feet. "This is Toby Houston, who's this?" As Andy and Jane watched, her face fell. "Oh, hi, Matt," she said. "Fine. Sure, hold on." She held out the phone to Andy.

"Hi!" Andy listened a minute, then said, "That would be fantastic!" Then her face fell. "Wait a sec, I've got to check on something." Putting her hand over the receiver, she turned to Jane and Toby. "Matt says the auditorium is free tomorrow morning. And I'm free, too, because my ten o'clock was canceled."

"So was mine," Toby said.

"Great! Because Matt and I want to work on my routine. And if you're free then, Toby, you can do something with Allegra."

Toby looked taken aback. "Well . . . I . . ."

"Come on, you saw last night how nice she is," Jane said. "I'd do it, but I made a late breakfast date with Cary. Besides, it'll be good — it'll take your mind off Max."

"What's wrong with Max?" Andy asked.

"Cough," Toby replied.

"Serious?"

"Don't know."

"Andy! You've got Matt on the line," Jane reminded her.

"Oh, right. Hang in there," Andy said into the phone. Turning back to Toby, she gave her a pleading look.

"Okay," Toby said. "I can't come up with a good excuse, and I know it's my turn, anyway."

Andy happily relayed the news to Matt, then hung up. "Thanks, Toby," she said. "And really, it won't be bad at all. Allegra's easy to talk to, you'll see. All you have to do is forget that she's a princess."

Forgetting that Allegra was a princess was about as easy as forgetting how to walk, Toby thought as Allegra joined her in the main hall of Baker House the next morning. As usual, when she was heading for Randy's, Toby wore jeans, an old plaid shirt, and her scruffy cowboy boots.

Allegra came down the stairs in cream colored jodhpurs, a white cotton shirt, and black leather, low-heeled riding boots that looked as soft as butter. She'd tied a sea-green silk scarf around her slender neck and pulled her dark hair back in a blue ribbon, so that her small gold earrings flashed in the sun.

Toby immediately felt like a second-class citizen.

"What a beautiful morning!" Allegra said as they set off toward the Crowells' farm. "I'm so glad you suggested riding, Toby. I love it. And it's one of the few things I can do without looking like I've got two left feet."

Toby licked her lips. It was obviously her turn to say something. "I guess riding is one of the things they teach you, huh? Like playing the piano and curtsying."

Allegra laughed. "Yes, exactly. Every well-brought-up princess should know how to sit a horse. When I was a little girl, I was terrified of the big beasts, but then I fed my first carrot to one of them, and I was in love."

Toby swallowed hard, remembering how much Max loved carrots, and the funny way he'd poke his velvety nose into her pockets to see if she'd brought him one. Stop it, she told herself. If you think about Max, you'll wind up mewling like a kitten. "I'm glad you know horses," she said, "but what about your . . . er . . ." she looked over her shoulder at Allegra's bodyguards.

"Oh, they can ride, too," Allegra assured

her. "In fact, I think they'll enjoy the exercise. I heard them complaining last night about too much sitting around." She shook her head. "I wanted to come on this tour without them, but I lost that battle. I hope your friend Mr. Crowell doesn't mind that they're with us."

"Oh, no, I told him," Toby said. "And you don't have to call him Mr. Crowell. Really. He'd probably wonder who you were talking to. His name's Randy."

"Randy," Allegra repeated. "That's a nice name. Short for Randolph?"

"I don't know," Toby admitted. "I never asked."

Randy was waiting for them when they arrived, and Toby was surprised to see that the whole paddock area had been spruced up. The weeds around the fence posts had disappeared, the loose railing was nailed firmly into place, and there were no empty grain sacks and moth-eaten horse blankets in sight.

Unsure of how to make the introductions, Toby hung back a little to give herself time. But the princess didn't have any problem. Holding out her hand, she walked straight up to Randy and smiled. "Hello. I'm Allegra, and I want to thank you for your hospitality. It's very kind of you to have me, and I'm very much looking forward to a good ride."

To Toby's amazement, Randy — cool, calm, collected Randy — blushed. "Well, you're welcome," he said, shaking Allegra's hand. "But . . . uh . . . the pleasure's all mine."

Allegra laughed. "Thank you. Shall we get started?"

Within minutes, the five of them were mounted and heading out of the paddock. Toby, Randy, and Allegra rode abreast for awhile, but soon Toby dropped behind. She didn't feel much like talking, and besides, Randy and the princess were getting along like two peas in a pod. Still brooding about Max, Toby let her horse plod along on its own. It wasn't until she felt her horse plunging downhill that she finally started paying attention to what was going on.

Ahead of her, Allegra and Randy were almost at the bottom of the ravine. They were riding side by side and still talking, his blond head leaning close to her dark one, his lips curving in a smile.

Suddenly, Randy's horse stumbled, and Toby almost shouted, "Watch it, you'll fall!" But the horse kept its balance easily, and Randy hadn't taken his eyes off Allegra.

That's when Toby realized that Randy had fallen — but not from his horse.

CHAPTER SEVEN

At dinner that night, Andy picked up her fork and made a few tentative pokes at the yellowish blob on her plate. "Are these noodles?"

"I certainly hope so," Jane said, swallowing quickly. "If they're not, don't tell me. I just ate some."

"Getting brave, aren't you?" Dee remarked.

"No, just starved," Jane said. "Studying hard always makes me ravenous."

"Me, too." Andy pushed the suspect noodles to the far side of her plate and tried some green beans. "Ugh. These things must have been boiled for an hour."

"Sure," Dee said. "That's rule number one in the Canby Hall cookbook — 'Cook It Till It's Dead.'" She laughed and then sighed. "Boy, I could sure go for a nice avocado salad. You'd think they could at least serve decent food here when everybody's studying for finals."

"That would ruin their reputation." Jane watched in awe as Toby forked up her last limp green bean and put it in her mouth. Her plate was now empty. "I can't believe you really ate all that," she commented quietly.

Toby swallowed and shrugged. "Hungry," she said, reaching for her milk.

"Oh, that's right." Andy gave up on the main course and went straight to the dessert. Canned fruit cocktail wasn't her favorite, but at least it was edible. "You worked up an appetite out on the open range this morning. I kept looking for you all day, but I didn't see you. How did it go? Was it fun?"

"It went fine," Toby said, not answering the second question.

"Is Allegra a good rider?" Dee asked. "I mean, did she pass your inspection?"

Another shrug. "She can sit a horse."

"Where is she, anyway?" Jane wondered.

"Probably smelled the dinner and decided to stay in her room," Andy joked.

"She's learning," Dee said. "By the time she leaves, she'll be a true Canby Hall girl — living on fruit juice and peanut butter crackers from the vending machine."

They were still joking about the food when Maggie Morrison bustled up to their table, her cheeks pink and her eyes shining behind her slightly smudged glasses. "Guess what?" she said excitedly.

"They canceled finals?" Dee asked.

"Better than that!"

"What could be better than that?" Andy wanted to know.

"Wait'll you hear," Maggie said. "I had to go buy some batteries for my Walkman, and when I was coming back, I passed by Pizza Pete's." She took a deep breath and grinned. "Guess who I saw going in there?"

"Pete?" Andy quipped.

Maggie shook her head. "Princess Allegra and Randy Crowell."

The others were silent for a moment. Then Dee grinned. "Looks like that horseback ride turned out to be real special."

"Isn't it neat?" Maggie said. "It's kind of like a movie or something, isn't it? This princess is engaged to a man she doesn't want to marry, and then she goes on a trip and falls in love."

"Who says they're in love?" Andy asked. "Going for a pizza together doesn't mean you're in love. Maybe they just became good friends. What about it, Toby? You were with them this morning, did you spot any budding romance?"

But Toby didn't answer. Sometime in the midst of all the talk, she'd quietly left the table.

Later, Andy and Jane went back to their room. Jane wanted to change before taking a walk with Cary, and Andy had decided to make a supreme sacrifice and spend the night studying. Both of them were thinking the same thing as they climbed the stairs.

"Maggie was right," Jane said, a slow smile spreading across her face. "If Randy and Allegra are really interested in each other, then it's just like a movie, or a fairy tale."

"I know," Andy agreed. "Allegra wanted a taste of real life, and she's sure going to get it now. But I can't help wondering how she plans to carry on a romance with those two stone-faced bodyguards following her around like shadows."

"I never thought of that," Jane said. "But she's probably so used to them, she doesn't even notice they're there."

"That's fine for her," Andy laughed. "But what about Randy?"

"Well, anyway, it'll be fun to see what happens."

"Mmm." Andy nodded. "Toby didn't seem too interested."

"Toby doesn't get very excited about fairy-tale romances," Jane said. "Besides, she's too miserable about that horse of hers to be interested in anything else right now."

Jane was wrong. As Toby stared into the wishing pond, which was where she'd hightailed it to after supper, she couldn't stop thinking about Randy.

What a dumb little Texas ninny she was. Secretly thinking it wouldn't be long before

Randy realized that the five years' difference in their ages didn't matter a whit. And what happens? Some princess comes from across the ocean and snatches him up before anybody can blink an eye.

And she was engaged, too, Toby thought, her anger turning against Allegra. She was practically married off to a fellow back home and here she was, two-timing him.

As for Randy, well, he was so far gone Toby didn't think he'd ever come back. What was all that talk about how gun-shy he was when it came to girls, just a bunch of hot air? He sure wasn't gun-shy around the princess. He'd done everything but ride his horse backwards to get her to smile.

Toby didn't know who she was mad at most — Randy, the princess, or herself. She scuffed the toe of her boot into the soft dirt by the pond and finally decided she was equally mad at all three.

Mostly, though, she was hurt. Randy was special to her; he made her feel a way nobody else ever had, not even Neal. And she'd been sure she was special to him, too, no matter what he'd said about her being too young. But there he was, making sheep's eyes at Princess Allegra, taking her to Pizza Pete's, probably kissing her good-night this very minute.

Restless and edgy, Toby picked up a rock and threw it into the wishing pond. It sank with a plop, just like her heart had sunk that morning. The only time she'd ever felt this bad since coming to Canby Hall was at the beginning of the year, when things were really rocky between her and Jane and Andy. That was the time she'd almost hopped the train and headed back home to Texas.

She felt bad enough now to do it again, but she knew she couldn't. She just couldn't turn tail and run, or everybody would know what a fool she was. And she was determined that nobody would know. Besides, she had to finish out the year, or she'd never be able to look her dad in the eye.

She might not be able to run away, but she *could* run, and that's exactly what she did. She ran straight back to Baker House, took the stairs two at a time, fished out her old army blanket, rolled up in it, and turned to the wall.

Andy, who had just paid a visit to the vending machine, came back into 407 and immediately noticed the gray-green lump on Toby's bed.

"Toby?" she said, poking the lump with her finger. "You sick?" Except for the time she'd sprained her ankle, Toby had never been to the infirmary.

"Nope."

"Cold?" It was almost seventy degrees outside.

"Nope."

"Sleepy?"

"Yep."

It was eight o'clock at night, but Andy decided not to mention that fact. Toby obviously didn't feel like talking, so Andy opened her package of cheese crackers as quietly as possible and went back to her books.

By the time Jane came in, Toby was fast asleep.

"Is she sick?" Jane whispered.

"Nope," Andy whispered back.

"Cold?"

"Nope."

"Then why does she have that blanket on?" Jane wanted to know. "Is she homesick?"

"Could be."

Jane rolled her eyes. "You sound just like her!"

"Just giving you some idea of the conversation I had with her an hour ago," Andy giggled. Then she stopped smiling. "She's upset, that's for sure. I mean, she's not the world's biggest talker, but when she starts communicating just in one-syllable words, you know something's wrong."

Jane let her sweater slip from her shoulders and drop to the floor. Pushing aside a pile of notebooks, she sat on her bed and nodded. "It's that horse," she said. "She's so worried about it, she can't even function. What kind of man is her father anyway? Writing her that the horse is sick and then not letting her know what's happening."

"According to Toby, he knows more about horses than anybody."

"Well, he may know horses, but he might need a few lessons in daughters," Jane said.

Just then, Toby sighed and rolled over in her sleep, one arm flopping off the side of the bed.

Her two roommates looked at her and then at each other. They both loved Toby, and when she hurt, they hurt. But they weren't sure how to help her, not when her problem was a thousand miles away on a ranch in Texas.

"I'm going to talk to her again tomorrow," Jane said. "She says she's scared to call and find out about Max, because she's afraid the news will be bad. But this is getting ridiculous!"

"Good idea," Andy agreed. "I'll put in my two cents worth, too."

Toby sighed again and muttered something.

"I guess I'll read some history," Jane whispered.

"Yeah, I've got to cram a few more facts into my head, too," Andy said.

For more than an hour, both girls studied. The dorm was strangely quiet; it seemed as if everyone had either left or had her head in a book. The phone was silent, and no one came in wanting to talk or to suggest a quick visit to the vending machines. It was a perfect atmosphere for studying, and by the time they shut their books, brushed their teeth, and turned off the lights, both Jane and Andy felt that they'd earned a good night's sleep.

At eleven-thirty, when Andy was just drift-ing off to sleep, she thought she heard a soft rapping at the door. Raising her head from the pillow, she listened again. Yes, there it was. Somebody was knocking.

As she was struggling out of her bed, Andy heard Jane start to stir. "What is it?" Jane mumbled groggily. "Do I have to get up already?"

Andy chuckled. "I'm surprised you even heard it," she said. "You're the original log when it comes to sleep."

"Hmm?" Jane's eyes were actually open now. "Who's banging on the door?"

"I'm just going to find out," Andy told her, slowly crossing the dark room. "Go back to sleep."

"I can't now," Jane complained, swinging her legs over the side of her bed. "Wait for me. I want to tell whoever it is that we're not interested."

Shuffling across the floor, Jane stubbed her toe on the corner of a bookcase. She was still hopping up and down, trying not to scream, when Andy opened the door.

In the dim light of the hall stood Allegra. Her dark hair spilled over the shoulders of her soft blue bathrobe, and her big eyes were bright.

"I'm sorry to disturb you," she said, seeing that they'd just awakened. "If you like, I'll go back to my room and talk to you in the morning."

"It's too late for that," Andy said with a smile. "I'd invite you in, but Toby's still asleep. Let's talk out here."

Andy and Jane stepped out into the hall, and Andy pulled the door softly shut. "What's up?" she asked. "You look like you're ready to burst."

"I am," Allegra said, her eyes shining even more. "I'm in love, and I need your help."

CHAPTER EIGHT

With whispers and giggles, the three girls made their way up to the fifth floor. They held their breath as they passed Meredith's door, and once inside Allegra's room, they burst out laughing.

"I'm still not sure why we're sneaking around like criminals," Jane said, as she sat down in the white wicker chair.

"Because all of this is a secret," Allerga told her.

"Are you kidding?" Andy laughed even harder. "We've known about it since dinner."

Allegra looked surprised. "How?" she asked. "I only found out myself this morning."

Jane told her about Maggie having seen the two of them. "But don't worry," she said. "Maggie won't tell anyone else if you don't want her to. I guess she didn't think it mattered."

"Oh, it doesn't really." Allegra flung herself on the bed and folded her arms underneath her head. "I'm too happy right now for anything to matter!" She laughed at the ceiling and then sat up. "I never thought I'd feel this way in my life! I never once thought I'd meet anyone like Randy, but when I went out this morning, there he was, waiting for me!"

"Sort of like a knight in shining armor?" Andy joked.

"Much better than that," Allegra said seriously. "Randy is real. And the best part is, he feels the same way about me." She flopped back on the bed again. "I never in a million years thought something this wonderful would happen to me."

As if to celebrate, she jumped off the bed, opened a desk drawer and brought out another box of rich chocolates. "Please, help yourselves," she said, and Jane's eyes lit up.

"Well, I hate to be the one to bring it up," Andy said, biting into a chocolate truffle. "But speaking of knights in shining armor, what about good old Prince Frederick?"

At the mention of Frederick, Allegra's face lost a little of its sparkle. "I don't want to think about him, but I suppose I'll have to sooner or later," she admitted. Then she grinned. "Let's make it later. I'm much too happy to think of him right at the moment, and besides, I really do need your help."

"With what?" Jane asked, reaching for another piece of candy.

"Yeah, it looks like you're doing just fine

without any help from anybody," Andy remarked.

"Two things," Allegra said. "One is my clothes."

"What's wrong with your clothes?" Jane asked, truly surprised. "You probably have the best wardrobe on campus."

"That's just it, it's a 'wardrobe,'" Allegra explained. "Everything's coordinated with everything else, and most of it's so stuffy and conventional." Turning to Andy, she went on, "I like the way you dress. You've got a great eye for color. Could you possibly loan me one of your tops for when I see Randy next?"

Andy was pleased. Before she'd met Allegra, she would have bet she'd go more for Jane's preppy look. But now she was beginning to see that underneath this proper princess, there was a normal girl trying to break out. "If you want the hip look, you've got it."

"Thanks. The hip look hasn't hit Montavia yet, or at least not the palace." Allegra lowered her voice. "That brings me to the second thing — my next date with Randy."

"Oh, I see," Jane said. "You want some suggestions on places to go."

Allegra shook her head. "No, we've already decided that. We're going riding in the morning, and then tomorrow night, a quick hamburger and a movie."

"Sounds great," Andy commented. "What's the problem?

"The problem is Joseph and Rodger."

Jane's hand paused over the chocolate box. "Who on earth are Joseph and Rodger?"

"The hulks," Andy said.

"The what?"

"The hulks — you know, the bodyguards."

"Yes, that's exactly what they remind me of," Allegra laughed. "Two hulking shadows. I really shouldn't laugh, though. They're very nice men, and they're good at watching out for me, although why they haven't died of boredom yet is beyond me. Anyway," she went on, "what Randy and I would really like is some privacy. I'm sure you understand."

Jane and Andy stared at the rug, imagining what it would be like trying to have a date with Matt or Cary while Joseph and Rodger hovered in the background.

"Yes," Jane said after a minute. "We understand."

"Well, then, I have an enormous favor to ask." Allegra took a deep breath. "If it's possible, would you mind helping me get a little free time with Randy? I mean completely free?"

"I wouldn't mind," Jane said slowly. "But I can't think of any way to do it except . . ."

"Except by helping you escape from Joe and Rodge," Andy finished for her.

"Exactly," Allegra said, her eyes gleaming. "That's exactly what I had in mind — an escape!"

* * *

"What do you think?" Jane whispered as she and Andy made their way down to the fourth floor a few minutes later. "Should we help her?"

"Well, she didn't ask us to do anything really crazy, like impersonating her or something," Andy said. "All she wants us to do is stand around so the two hulks think we're waiting for her. She said she'd take care of the rest of it."

"Yes, and she doesn't expect them not to find her," Jane went on. "But while they're looking, she and Randy can have a little time by themselves."

"And it's not as if she'll be in any danger," Andy said as they walked toward 407. "If Randy's as crazy about her as she is about him, he'll make sure she doesn't even stub her toe."

Jane put her hand on the doorknob, and then smiled. "It looks like we've decided to help her."

"Right," Andy said. "Every true romance deserves help. Besides, think how much fun it'll be!"

Stifling their laughter, they opened the door. A shaft of light from the hallway fell across Toby's face, and she opened her eyes a crack.

"Sorry," Jane whispered. "Go back to sleep."

"What's going on?" Toby asked.

"Nothing," Andy said, yawning. "Just a

little meeting with Allegra. Go back to sleep."

Toby's eyes opened wider. "The princess?" she asked. "What'd she want?"

As Jane threw back her covers, four notebooks fell off, their plastic covers hitting the floor with a slap. "Once I found out Allegra was human, I stopped worrying about the way my part of the room looked," she commented. "It's too bad. It was much nicer when it was neat."

"It sure was," Andy remarked. "Maybe we'll get lucky, and a duchess will decide to visit next."

"What did the princess want?" Toby repeated.

"Oh, right. Allegra." Andy slid between her sheets and stretched her legs. "She asked us if we'd help her find some private time with Randy."

"That's right," Jane said, punching her pillow. "We're going to try to give them half an hour alone together, without the bodyguards breathing down their necks." She yawned loudly. "What about it, Toby? Do you want to join us in the conspiracy?"

But Toby had rolled herself in the army blanket again. And once again, she was facing the wall.

"All right, this is it," Andy said tensely. "What do we do if we're caught — give our name, rank, and serial number?"

"Don't be ridiculous." Jane looked calm

and collected as usual, but underneath she was as tense with anticipation as Andy. "All Allegra asked us to do was wait here in the main hall. And if the bodyguards ask us if we've seen her, we're supposed to say no. Which will be the truth."

It was nine-fifteen the next morning. As promised, Jane and Andy were ready to help the princess with her first "escape" from the ever-watchful eyes of Joseph and Rodger. Allegra had insisted that they not run the risk of getting in trouble themselves, so she hadn't told them exactly what her plan was. All they knew was that they were supposed to stay in the main hall and wait.

The two bodyguards were standing just outside the front doors, hands in their pockets, peering inside every once in a while. They must have been told to wait, too, and from the way they looked at Jane and Andy, it was obvious they thought the princess would be joining them.

"I'm beginning to feel very conspicuous," Andy said. "I mean, how often do we just hang out in the main hall twiddling our thumbs?"

"Stop feeling guilty," Jane said. "Why would anyone be suspicious of us?"

As if on cue, Ms. Allardyce walked through the front entrance and glanced around as if taking inventory. When she saw Jane and Andy, she frowned and walked over to them.

"Good morning, girls," she said. "Is everything all right?"

"Oh, yes, everything's fine," Jane told her.

"Couldn't be better," Andy added.

"Well, I'm glad to hear it," the headmistress said. "It's nice to know you have so much free time on your hands, considering the fact that finals aren't very far off."

"Well, we're not really all that free," Andy said. Jane shot her a warning glance but Andy ignored it. "Princess Allegra asked us to wait here," she went on, "and we didn't want to disappoint her, even though we do have a ton of studying to do."

"Oh, yes, the princess," Ms. Allardyce said approvingly. "Charming girl. How do you think she likes Canby Hall so far?"

"As far as I can tell, she's fallen in love," Andy replied.

This time, Jane didn't dare catch Andy's eye. If she had, she wouldn't have been able to keep a straight face.

"Why that's wonderful news!" Ms. Allardyce positively beamed with satisfaction. "I knew I'd made the right choice when I picked you girls to be her hostesses. I trust October is doing her part, too?"

"Oh, of course," Jane said. "She took the princess riding yesterday, and it turned out to be one of the best times Allegra has ever had."

"Good, good," the headmistress said. "Well,

I'll leave you to your waiting. Give my regards to the princess, and tell her I plan to have her to tea once more before she leaves."

"We sure will," Andy said.

With a pleased smile, Ms. Allardyce finally left them.

Jane, who'd been standing stiff as a board, almost collapsed with relief. "I couldn't believe you said that about Allegra falling in love with Canby Hall!" she said. "You really like to live dangerously, don't you?"

"You've got to admit, it's exciting," Andy laughed. "Anyway, I didn't say she was in love with Canby Hall. I just said she was in love, and that's the truth. Besides, you should talk — what about when you told her how fantastic the horseback riding was?"

"You're right," Jane admitted. "I just couldn't resist it." She laughed, too, and then glanced outside. "Look. Isn't that Randy's truck?"

"The one and only," Andy said, as Randy's old pick-up drove past the entrance. "I wonder what the deal is? If they're trying to make a getaway, they're sure not being very sneaky about it."

At that moment, a piercing scream echoed through Baker House. Even though Jane and Andy had been warned, they both jumped a foot off the ground.

For about three seconds, the dorm was completely silent, as if everyone had been paralyzed by the shriek. Then, pandemonium broke loose.

Footsteps thundered on the floor, and a group of girls came dashing in from the study room, their faces white and their eyes wide. "What was that?" one of them cried out. "I don't know," another one said, "but I think it came from the princess's room!"

Ms. Allardyce, accompanied by Meredith, rushed in from the dining hall. They weren't panicked, but they were obviously worried. The scream had been so shattering, so ear-splitting, that everyone naturally assumed that something horrible had happened.

"Stop!" Merry cried out to another group of girls coming down the stairs. "Who screamed and why and where is she?"

"I don't know, but it came from the fifth floor!" a girl answered. "I was afraid to go up by myself, but I'll come with you if you want!"

"I do want," Merry replied, and she bounded up the steps in her sneakers, way ahead of Ms. Allardyce, who was wearing heels.

It wasn't long before the two bodyguards had been alerted to the scream, and where it had come from. Moving swiftly and eagerly, as if they welcomed some action, they strode into the main hall and swept up the stairs like two panthers.

In the middle of the turmoil, Jane and Andy

stood their ground, looking worried and concerned, but not budging an inch.

"This is silly," Jane said finally. "I feel like a complete dolt."

"Yeah? Well, take a look outside," Andy suggested.

Jane looked, just in time to see Randy's truck disappearing down the drive. Even from this distance, she could see that there were two people in it this time.

"If you feel like a dolt," Andy laughed, "how do you think Joe and Rodge are going to feel when they find out Allegra's flown the coop?"

CHAPTER NINE

Ten minutes later, Meredith and Ms. Allardyce came back down the steps, this time accompanied by a girl whose face was scarlet with embarrassment.

"Who's that?" Andy asked.

"I don't know her name," Jane said. "I think she's from Addison House."

"I didn't mean to scream," the girl was telling Meredith and the headmistress, "but it looked so real when I first saw it." She giggled and blushed again. "Of course, once I took a second look, I knew what it was, but by then it was too late."

"Yes, yes, we understand," Ms. Allardyce said, looking extremely annoyed at having had to make such an undignified dash up the stairs. "Of course you do realize that you don't find such things in Massachusetts?"

"Uh, no, I didn't know that," the girl stammered. "I'm from Florida."

"Hmm. Remind me to give you a book on insect life in New England," Ms. Allardyce said as the two of them went outside.

"What on earth were they talking about?" Jane wondered.

"We're about to find out," Andy said. "Here comes Meredith."

The corners of her mouth twitching in amusement, the housemother approached the two roommates. "I never thought I'd see Patrice Allardyce take the stairs two at a time," she commented. "Actually, she got up faster than I thought she would."

"What happened?" Andy asked.

Merry laughed. "That poor girl — Cindy — collects autographs and she wanted Princess Allegra's. So she came over early this morning to get it. But before she knocked, she happened to glance down at the floor, and she saw this."

Merry brought her hand out from behind her back and held up a hideous black furry spider, about the size of a saucer. Up close, it was obviously a fake, but from a distance, it must have looked very real.

"So she screamed," Andy said.

"Did she ever!" Merry laughed. "I told her she could probably get a job in a horror film any time she wanted. What surprises me is that the princess didn't come rushing out. She must be a very heavy sleeper."

At that moment, Joseph and Rodger reappeared, their faces stonier than ever. When they saw Jane and Andy, they made a beeline for them.

"Princess Allegra's not with you?" one of them asked.

"No," Jane said. "She's not."

"She told us to wait downstairs for her," the other one said, his blank expression changing to worry. "We saw you two and thought you were all going somewhere together."

"No, we didn't have any plans for this morning," Andy told them.

"I thought she was still in her room," Meredith said. The two bodyguards shook their heads. "Then maybe she's in the dining hall."

"We just looked. She's not."

"Oh . . . well. . . ." Meredith looked confused but when she glanced at Andy and Jane, the confusion disappeared. Her eyes bright with suspicion, she said, "You two wouldn't happen to know where she is, by any chance?"

"Yes, we do," Jane said.

Joseph and Rodger spoke together. "Where?"

"She said she was going riding with Randy Crowell," Andy told them. "You were there yesterday, remember? It's that horse farm a little way out of town? The one with the big red barn?"

But Joseph and Rodger had already left.

Meredith looked at the two roommates and shook her head. "How much time did all this confusion get her?"

"About half an hour," Jane said, checking her watch.

"And was it really worth it?" Meredith asked.

"Allegra thinks so," Andy said.

"I'm not going to ask why she planned this elaborate getaway because I think I've guessed." Meredith said. "When someone goes through this just for thirty minutes' free time with a boy, then obviously that boy is very special to her."

Jane and Andy nodded, as if they'd both just come to the same conclusion.

"But those two security men have a job to do," Meredith pointed out. "Fortunately, they're not employed by Canby Hall, so you're not really breaking any of the school's rules." She shook her head again. "But you're breaking *their* rules, so don't get too carried away. If I were you, I wouldn't want to wind up on their bad side."

Once started, though, the romance between "The Princess and the Farmboy," as it came to be called, couldn't be stopped. It couldn't be kept a secret, either, because Allegra was so happy, she discovered that she couldn't keep quiet about it and told everyone who'd listen how wonderful it was.

There was almost no one who didn't want to listen, either. As far as Allegra was concerned, she was getting a taste of real life. But to everyone else, the idea of a princess falling in love with a local boy was slightly unreal. As Maggie had said, it was like a movie, and most girls were completely enchanted with the script.

Once the news was out, Allegra had plenty of volunteers offering to help her with more getaways. But, like Meredith, she didn't want anyone getting on the bad side of her bodyguards, so she planned her escapes by herself. That first night, after the movies, she and Randy had almost finished an entire pizza before Joseph and Rodger discovered where she'd gone. And the next day, they were able to spend forty-five minutes alone in the country before the bodyguards crashed their picnic.

Allegra's plan was simple. She always told one girl where she was going, and when. Then, when Joseph and Rodger started asking about her, the girl would let them know. By that time, of course, the happy couple had usually been gone for at least half an hour. There were no more screams at fake spiders, which had been a lucky mistake — Allegra had bought it as a souvenir and accidentally dropped it. But somehow, she always managed to disappear just when she wanted to, and some of the girls started keeping a record of how long she'd have before she was discovered.

It was a game, really, and everyone enjoyed it, especially Allegra. She didn't get upset when the bodyguards showed up; instead, she

teased them about how long they'd taken.
Joseph and Rodger caught on to the game
very fast, and though their faces stayed as
rock-like as ever, Andy thought she saw
Rodger's eyes twinkling once.

"I don't believe it," Jane laughed, when
Andy reported it to her. "The only person
less cheerful than those two guys is Toby."
Then, realizing what she'd said, she stopped
laughing. "Where is Toby, anyway? I haven't
seen her except at night, and then she's always
rolled up in that blanket like a cowboy at a
campfire."

"I think she's been spending a lot of time
at the library," Andy said. "I saw her there
yesterday, anyway."

"Did you talk?"

"Sort of." Andy shrugged. "I said 'hi,' and
she said 'hi.' I said 'how's it going?' and she
said 'okay.'"

"Still communicating mostly in words of
one syllable," Jane sighed. "We've been so
busy with the great romance, we've sort of
forgotten about her. I think it's about time
we did something to cheer her up."

"Like what?" Andy asked. "The only thing
that'll cheer her up is good news about Max."

"You're right." Jane's eyes started to sparkle
as she thought of something. "Listen, she's
afraid to call home and find out what's going
on. But we're not afraid, are we?"

"We're not?"

"No, we're not," Jane said firmly. "Barretts

are not cowards, and neither are Cords. Neither are Houstons; it's just that Toby's too involved. Anyway," she went on, "we'll call Mr. Houston for her. And if Max is all right, she won't have to wait any longer to find out."

"Let's just hope he *is* all right."

"I'm sure he is," Jane said confidently. "I'm just positive that he's as healthy as a . . ."

"As a horse?" Andy finished with a grin.

"Exactly."

Later that evening, when Allegra was out with Randy, and Toby had silently departed for the library, Jane and Andy quickly went down the hall to the phone where they could make an outgoing call.

"What's the number?" Jane said, picking up the receiver.

"I thought you knew," Andy told her.

"I thought *you* did."

Andy laughed. "Never mind. Call information. How many phones could there be in Rattlesnake Creek, anyway?"

Jane got the operator, and Andy must have been right about the number of phones in that part of Texas, because she had the number in about two seconds. "Here goes," Jane said, dialing. "Think positive thoughts."

On the third ring, the phone was picked up, and a man said hello.

"Mr. Houston?" Jane said.

"Speaking."

His voice was dry, and calm, and even more

"Texas" than Toby's, which Jane hadn't thought possible. "Mr. Houston, my name is Jane Barrett and I'm a roommate of Toby's," she said. "Before I say anything else, though, I want to assure you that Toby's fine. This isn't an emergency call."

"Glad to hear it," he replied.

There was a pause. Jane thought he might ask her why she was calling, but obviously he was waiting for her to tell him. "Yes, well," she went on, "Toby's fine physically, but she is awfully worried about something."

"Beg pardon?"

The connection was very good, Jane thought. Toby's father must be hard of hearing. Raising her voice, she said, "Worried. Toby's very worried."

"No need to shout." There was a dry chuckle. "I apologize, but I'm having a little trouble with your accent."

"Oh, I see."

"What's he saying?" Andy asked.

"My accent," Jane told her, covering the phone and raising her eyebrows. "Imagine. He thinks I have an accent."

Andy took a few steps away so she could laugh out loud at Jane's expression.

"Go on, young lady," Mr. Houston said. "I got it finally. Toby's worried. What's she botherin' her head about?"

"She's bothering her head . . . er . . . she's worried about Max," Jane said.

"Max?"

"Yes, her horse. Max."

"Shoot, why?"

Jane frowned. Didn't he know? "Well, she mentioned something about a letter you wrote, telling her Max had a cough."

There was another silence, and Jane was just about to repeat what she'd said, when Mr. Houston chuckled again, longer and louder this time. "If that doesn't beat all!" he said. "Here I was, struggling to think of some news to write, and I say the first thing that comes to mind and it backfires on me!"

"I'm afraid I don't understand," Jane said.

"Didn't expect you to," he replied. "Toby's got two Maxes in her life — a horse and an uncle from her mother's side. Her Uncle Max had a cough, and I wrote her about it, fool that I was."

"And the other Max?" Jane asked, ignoring Andy's confused stare.

"The horse? Shoot, he's kickin' up his heels. Thinks he's a colt again. He's a bigger fool than I am." Another chuckle.

"That's wonderful news, Mr. Houston. And Uncle Max?" Jane asked politely. "How is he?"

"Just like the horse. Fit as a fiddle. You tell Toby to stop frettin'."

"I'll do that right away," Jane told him. "Thank you, Mr. Houston. I hope I didn't disturb your evening."

"Didn't bother me a bit," he said cheerfully. "It was a pleasure talkin' with you, Miss Barrett."

"Well?" Andy asked, when Jane finally hung up. "I figured out that Max is all right, but what about Uncle Max? Did he pull through?"

"Both Maxes are doing beautifully," Jane said happily. "It was just a case of mistaken identity. Come on, let's go tell Toby!"

They found Toby in her latest hangout, the library, pouring over an English book and looking miserable.

"Guess what!" Jane whispered excitedly.

"Yeah," Andy said, "have we got news for you!"

Toby propped her chin in her hand and stared at them. "What is it?"

"Max is fine!" Jane almost shouted. Several heads turned to stare, so she lowered her voice. "He was always fine. He's fit as a colt . . . no, he's kicking like a fiddle . . . well, whatever healthy horses do!" she finished.

Toby took her hand away and her mouth dropped open. "How do you know?"

"Now don't get mad," Andy said. "But we just got tired of seeing you walking around with your chin dragging the ground, so we called your dad."

Toby's eyes widened. "You called Rattlesnake Creek?"

"Yes, thanks to the wonders of modern communication, we didn't have to send a stagecoach with a message," Jane said. "Anyway, your father said when he wrote you that letter, he was talking about your Uncle Max. On your mother's side. Remember him?"

"Sure, but — "

"I know, he forgot to mention that, and you just naturally thought he was talking about the horse." Jane laughed. "Your father's a very nice man, Toby, even though he does think I've got an accent."

"Anyway, both Maxes are fine, and the horse variety never even had a cough," Andy said. "What do you say about that?"

Toby shook her head, her mouth curving in its first smile in two days. "Shoot."

"Exactly what your father said," Jane told her. "He also said for me to tell you to stop frettin'."

"So come on, let's go back to Baker House and raid the candy machine to celebrate," Andy suggested.

"I've got a better idea," Jane said. "Allegra will probably be back pretty soon from her date. Let's wait for her and have a quick party."

"Great," Andy said. "I'm dying to find out what kind of runaround she gave the hulks tonight. What do you say, Toby, are you with us?"

"Uh, no, I better not," Toby said quickly. "Got to study some more."

"But — "

"Thanks for finding out about Max for

me." Toby smiled a second time. "I mean it. You two are the best. But I just can't party tonight." Turning back to the table, she bent her head over the English book. The smile had left her face so quickly that Andy and Jane wondered if they'd imagined it.

One thing they weren't imagining, though, one thing they knew for sure, was that Toby was still fretting. Only this time, it wasn't about Max.

CHAPTER
TEN

After Jane and Andy left, Toby closed her book and rested her chin in her hand again. It was almost closing time at the library, and girls were gathering their books, shuffling papers, and talking loudly as they got ready to go. Toby stared straight ahead, not noticing any of it.

Max is fine, she told herself. Like Jane said, he's always been fine. You should be hollering with joy. Not only is your horse fine and dandy, but you have two friends who cared enough to call and find out about him when you were too scared to.

But glad as Toby was about Max, the minute Jane and Andy said Allegra's name, any happy hollers died in her throat.

It just isn't fair, she said to herself for about the hundredth time. Never mind that Princess Allegra was already engaged. With her looks, she could have had her pick of just about any boy she met. And who did she have to go and pick but Randy Crowell. The one boy Toby wanted to be picked by. Maybe not now, maybe not next year, but some time. And now, all because of the princess, it would never happen.

"Excuse me, October."

Toby looked up and saw the round worried eyes of Ms. Phelps, the librarian, staring down at her. "The closing bell has rung twice, and you didn't budge. I was afraid you might be ill."

"Uh, no ma'am," Toby said, getting her books together. "I was just thinking hard."

"Well, that's good to see," Ms. Phelps said approvingly. "Especially at this time of year. Good luck on your finals."

"Oh, finals." In spite of the hours spent in the library, Toby didn't think she'd learned much. "Yes, thank you, Ms. Phelps."

The last bell rang, and as Toby stepped out of the library into the balmy spring night, she filled her lungs with the fresh air and for a few seconds, felt good again. Being inside that library hours at a time had made her very sympathetic to animals in cages. For Toby, who had grown up with acres of Texas ranchland as her playground, closed spaces were hard to take at the best of times, which meant they were almost impossible to take now.

Always before, when things got rough, or the dorm walls seemed to be closing in, or the pretty, tree-covered campus of Canby Hall just felt too crowded, Toby would take off for the Crowell farm. And then she'd ride, sometimes alone, but most times with Randy. It wasn't the ranch, of course. There weren't any views, for one thing, because there were too many hills. And there weren't any dried out gullies, or flat-topped mesas, or red-orange suns that sank quickly in the west, draining the wide-open sky of color as they went down.

But there was room to breathe. And there were horses. And there was Randy.

Now, though, there wasn't any of that, and Toby had no place to go but back to Baker House.

Well, she thought, trudging toward the dorm as slowly as possible, that wasn't quite true. She'd gotten a letter from Neal the day before, inviting her to spend a few days at his parents' house in Boston after finals and before she went home. He'd promised to take her sailing, which she'd never done, and he'd also said he'd give her "plenty of fresh air and not put her through more than one big family gathering" the whole time she was there.

It sounded like fun, but Toby had already decided to say no. How could she go to Boston, feeling the way she did? She'd just mope around and ruin everything. Much better to go home, feed Max some carrots, and spend about a month not talking to anybody.

* * *

Back at Baker House, Andy and Jane went into Room 407 and flopped down on their respective beds. Both of them felt as deflated as punctured balloons.

"What did we do wrong?" Jane asked after a minute. "She didn't seem mad that we'd called her father. And she actually smiled when we gave her the news about Max. I didn't expect her to turn handsprings in the library, but I thought she'd at least crack one of her Texas jokes and be the old Toby again. What did we do wrong?"

"We didn't do anything wrong," Andy said, lifting first one leg and then the other. She was going to practice her dance routine in the morning and she hadn't exercised all day. "Something else has been bothering her all along. If it had just been Max, then she would have turned back into the old Toby. So what we have to do now is find out what that something else is."

"How are we going to do that?" Jane asked, sitting up and pulling off her sandals. "Talking to her these days is like talking to a rock."

"We're just gonna have to lasso the filly," Andy drawled, "set on her, and not budge till she tells us what's wrong."

"Okay," Jane laughed. "I'll do the sitting. Can you handle a rope?"

"Shoot," Andy went on in her imitation Texas accent, "I can hogtie anything that moves."

"Hello." Princess Allegra, wearing one of

Andy's tops — a geometric print in vivid blue and gold — stuck her head around the door. "May I come in for a moment?"

"Sure," Andy said. "We were just hanging out."

With a sigh, the princess came into the room and plopped a box down on Jane's desk. "I'm out of French chocolates," she said. "But I do have these water biscuits. Will they do? I need to talk."

"You don't have to bring food to talk to us, you know," Andy said. "I'm about to get insulted."

"Please don't," Allegra told her, smiling a little. "I know I don't need to bring anything, but I also know that Jane likes to eat."

"I didn't realize it was so obvious," Jane said, slitting the cellophane wrapper with her thumbnail. "Andy's right, of course, you can come empty-handed any time." She laughed and pulled out a thin cracker. "But I do love water biscuits."

"Now that that's all clear, what's up?" Andy asked. "You don't look like somebody who's madly in love. You look miserable."

"I'm both," Allegra said, sitting on Toby's bed.

"Well, we know why you're in love," Jane commented. "Now tell us why you're miserable."

"Because this is Thursday," Allegra said, as if it should be obvious. "And tomorrow's Friday."

"Right. And then comes . . . oh." Andy stopped and shook her head. "Saturday's your last day."

Allegra nodded. "I have exactly two days before I have to leave Canby Hall, leave my new friends, and especially, leave Randy." She sighed again, and her dark, long-lashed eyes filled with tears. "What am I going to do?"

It was too soon to say anything. Jane was sympathetic but always uncomfortable with displays of emotion, so she busied herself by opening the can of soda she'd bought on the way back and handed it to Allegra. Andy put a box of tissues within easy reach, patted Allegra on the shoulder, lay down on the floor, and started some sit-ups.

In a few seconds, the tears slowed. Allegra blew her nose, wiped her eyes, took a sip of soda, and then started crying all over again. Finally, she stopped for good. "Oh," she said, blowing her nose again. "I never realized this would happen. If I'd known, I would never have come here."

"I don't believe that for a minute," Andy said gently. "You mean you'd really give up what you've had with Randy these past few days?"

"No, I suppose not," Allegra admitted. "But what am I going to do now? I can't stay here. The only place I have to go is home, and all that's waiting for me there is Frederick."

"Is he so terrible?" Jane asked.

"No, he's not terrible at all, as far as I can tell," Allegra said. "But that's not the point. The point is, he's not Randy."

"Speaking of Randy," Andy said, touching her elbows to her knees, "how's he taking all this?"

"Like a prince," Allegra said and almost laughed. "I mean that he hasn't put any pressure on me. He knows my situation, and he says that whatever I do, he'll never stop caring for me. He's been wonderful," she went on, her voice quavering. "But I can tell that he's miserable, too. We're both just completely lost. We don't know what to do."

It wasn't a problem with an easy solution. Playing dumb while Allegra snuck off with Randy was child's play. But now, Jane and Andy realized that the game everyone had enjoyed so much was over. The game had been a fanstasy, and it was easy; now they had to face reality, and it was hard.

"Well, look at it this way," Andy said, brightening up. "There's always next year. Summer vacation is only three months long, and then you'll be back at Canby Hall, and everything'll be fine again." She sat up and grinned. "You *are* going to pick Canby Hall, aren't you?"

"Of course," Allegra said.

"Then Andy's right," Jane told her. "Those three months will fly by, you'll see. You and

Randy can write to each other every day, and
when school starts up, everything will be
back to the way it was."

The princess thoughtfully nibbled a
cracker. Then she shook her head. "No."

"But why?" Andy asked. "That was the
deal you made with your family, right? You
get to come to the United States for a year,
or you won't marry Fred."

"Actually," Allegra said, "the deal was that
I come to the United States for a year and
then I marry Fred."

"Oh." Jane thought a second. "Well, things
can change a lot in a year."

"Yes, and that's exactly what my family's
afraid of. Once they find out about Randy, I
may not even get to come back next year."

"Who's going to tell them about Randy?"
Andy asked.

"Joseph and Rodger. Oh, not to be mean,
but they will be required to give a report on
how I spent my time." She laughed a little.
"I'm afraid my little escapes aren't going to
sound so funny when Rodger and Joseph
mention them."

For a moment, Allegra looked like she
might cry again, but she stopped herself.
"Enough," she said. "I'm not going to cry like
a baby anymore. Not tonight, anyway." Slid-
ing off Toby's bed, she accidentally pulled
the army blanket to the floor. She put it back,
frowning a little as she smoothed out the

wrinkles. "Toby doesn't like me, does she?" she asked suddenly.

Jane was surprised. "Why do you say that?"

"She seems to avoid me."

"She's been avoiding most people lately," Andy said, feeling a little uncomfortable discussing their friend while she wasn't there. "She . . . she's been studying a lot. She decided to get spectacular grades this semester, and once Toby decides something, that's it."

Allegra nodded. "Randy told me that. He said he liked her stubbornness."

"He talked about Toby?" Jane asked.

"Oh, yes. He said the first time he met her, she threw herself on to the back of a wild horse and stopped it from running away. They've been great friends ever since."

"They do a lot together," Jane said slowly, as if she'd just realized it. "Randy saved her life once."

"Yes, he told me about that," Allegra said. "He said they're very close, sort of like brother and sister. That's why I thought Toby and I might get along, too." She thought a moment. "But maybe it's my fault. I've been too caught up in Randy to pay much attention to anyone else."

"Maybe," Andy said doubtfully.

"Well, anyway, thank you for the tissues and the talk," Allegra said, going to the door. "Jane, the water biscuits are all yours."

When the princess had gone, Jane and Andy

stared at each other for a long time. Finally,
Andy broke the silence. "Are you thinking
what I'm thinking?"

"If we're thinking the same thing," Jane
said, "then we must be feeling the same way."

"Like skunks?"

"Exactly."

They both sighed. "But I thought Toby
had gotten over Randy!" Jane said.

"If she did, she didn't tell me about it,"
Andy remarked. "Of course, she didn't tell
me there was anything to get over in the first
place. I kind of figured that one out for myself."

"So did I. But I really thought that was
behind her, especially after she and Neal
started getting along so well."

"Maybe Toby thought so, too, and then
Allegra came along and she realized it wasn't
behind her." Andy groaned. "And here we've
been babbling away about this great romance,
and helping Allegra get away from the bodyguards, and all the time Toby's been miserable."

Jane straightened up, squared her shoulders, and reached for the crackers. "Well, we
shouldn't keep feeling guilty about that,"
she said firmly. "If Toby didn't know how she
felt about Randy, then how were we supposed to know? Besides, guilt doesn't get anything done, and we have to do something.
The question is what?" She bit into a cracker
and chewed for a moment, thinking hard.

"How about if we wipe out the last five days?" Andy suggested after a minute. "Turn back the clock and rewrite the script?"

"That would be nice," Jane said. "But how would you rewrite it so that everybody would be happy?"

"Simple. I'd make Allegra crazy about Fred."

"Where would that leave Randy?"

"Oh, right," Andy said. "Well, I'd just write him out of the picture."

"Toby wouldn't like that," Jane pointed out.

"Right again," Andy agreed. "I guess it's not that easy to come up with a happy ending."

They both laughed and then looked at each other again. "I guess I know what we have to do," Andy said.

Jane nodded. "We have to talk to Toby."

"Well, here I am," Toby said from the doorway. "Go ahead and talk."

CHAPTER ELEVEN

Piling her books on the desk, Toby sat on her bed, pulled off her boots and then scooted back against the wall, her arms around her knees. "Talk," she said again.

Jane spent a lot of time clearing her throat and trying to decide how to start, but Andy plunged right in. "Listen," she said. "I know we've been acting like we've got cement instead of brains between our ears, but we finally figured it out."

Toby's green eyes were confused. "Figured what out?"

"Why you're acting the way you are."

"How's that?" Toby asked.

"Wretched," Jane said bluntly. "We thought it was Max, but now we know we were wrong. Not that you weren't worried about him, but there was something else bothering you, too."

Neither Jane nor Andy was eager to mention Randy's name, and they were hoping that Toby would do it first. Instead, Toby just nodded. "Maybe," she said. Then she got up, peeled off her jeans, took off her shirt, and put on the big blue Lone Star State T-shirt she slept in.

Her two roommates watched her in silence.

"Well," Andy finally said in frustration, as Toby folded the army blanket at the foot of the bed, "don't you want to talk about it?"

"Nope." Toby slid between the rainbow-covered sheets.

"But, Toby . . ." Jane started to say.

"I never did understand why everybody thinks talk is so great," Toby interrupted. "Talk just causes trouble, to my way of thinkin.' "

"You know that's not true," Jane said.

Toby lifted her head. "It may not be true in Boston or Greenleaf, but it sure is true in Rattlesnake Creek. We manage to solve our problems out there without talkin' them to death."

"But, Toby," Andy said, "we just want to help."

"I know," Toby said. "And I know you mean well. But if you really want to help, you'll let me get to sleep." And she put an end to the conversation by turning on her side, her face to the wall.

Shaking their heads, Jane and Andy exchanged glances. Then they smiled. Both were thinking the same thing again — Toby can't

shut us up that easily. We'll try again tomorrow.

But the next day, Toby was up and out of the
dorm before anyone else had her eyes open.
No one knew where she'd gone, and the sign-
out sheet simply said, "Greenleaf."

That didn't exactly narrow it down, Andy
thought as she read it after a quick breakfast
of toast and apple juice. She knew Toby had
a ten o'clock class; she'd be back for that. Or
maybe she wouldn't, considering her mood.
Anyway, Andy couldn't wait for her. She
had to meet Matt and go through the routine
again. The audition was coming up soon, and
the worst part wasn't even the audition. The
worst part was that she'd have to wait till
August, when they sent out the students'
class schedules, to find out if she'd made it.

You're going to make it, Andy told herself.
Pushing Toby to the back of her mind for
the moment, she hitched her canvas bag a
little higher on her shoulder, shoved open the
front door of Baker House and headed for
the auditorium.

Forty-five minutes later, the phone rang in
Room 407. Jane, whose eleven o'clock class
had been canceled so they could spend the
time studying, turned over in bed and tried
to work the ringing sound into the dream
she was having. It was a lovely dream — she
was walking around Louisburg Square at sun-
set. It was quiet and peaceful, and she was

feeling extremely happy. Unfortunately, a ringing telephone didn't fit in anywhere, and she finally woke up.

Yawning widely, she fumbled for the phone and managed to croak out a hello.

"Good morning, bright eyes!"

"Cary?"

"The one and only," he said. "I hope I didn't disturb your morning workout."

"Very funny." Jane yawned again and ran her fingers through her hair. "I'm glad you called, but why'd you call so early?"

"Early?" Cary laughed. "It's almost ten."

"Why aren't you in class?"

"For the same reason you're not. I love the two weeks before finals, don't you, with classes being canceled right and left? The teachers think we'll use the time to study, but we know better, don't we?"

"We do?"

"Sure. Before we study, we'll eat," Cary said. "How about breakfast at the Greaf? I'll be your personal waiter."

The mention of breakfast made Jane's stomach rumble. "I'll be there in half an hour," she said.

"Great. I need your advice about something, so make sure you're awake," Cary teased. "And by the way, just so you'll know me, I'll wear a rose in my buttonhole."

Laughing, Jane hung up, showered quickly, and dressed in a white blouse and a pair of tan walking shorts. She wondered what kind of advice Cary could need, but mostly she wondered about Toby. She'd never seen Toby so unhappy, and it was frustrating, not knowing what to do for her. If only she'd open up and talk, she just might feel better.

In spite of what Toby had said, Jane wasn't a big fan of talking things out. Usually she believed that people should solve their problems by themselves. Dragging others into it just wasn't in good taste. But this was different. Toby probably thought she could handle everything just fine, without bothering anyone. What she was really doing was not handling it at all.

As she passed by the desk, Jane saw the word "Greenleaf" in Toby's bold handwriting on the sign-out sheet. Then she saw that Toby had come back, signing in at nine-thirty. She'll go to her classes and then to the library, Jane thought, deciding she'd try to find her that afternoon. Like Andy, Jane pushed Toby to the back of her mind. Then she walked out into the sunshine to go meet Cary.

But Toby wasn't in the library, or in class. Instead, she was at the tennis courts. Her geometry class had been a review of stuff they'd need to know for the finals, and people were free to leave whenever they wanted to. Toby decided she wanted to midway through. That left her with forty-five minutes before her next class. She couldn't face setting foot in the library yet, so she got her racket and headed for the tennis court. It wasn't the ranch, but at least it didn't have four walls.

The courts were popular these days. Even girls who didn't play well came to them for a break in studying. Dee Williams, who did play well, spotted Toby immediately and asked her to play.

"The best two out of three?" Dee asked.

"You're on," Toby said. As she walked to her side of the court, she remembered why she'd taken this game up in the first place — so she could impress Randy and play with him.

Then, with a shake of her head, Toby sent that memory flying. She'd started out to impress Randy, and she'd hated the game. But once she got the hang of it, she'd started playing for herself and not for anybody else. Do that right now, she ordered herself. Just play for yourself.

For twenty minutes, Toby played for herself, and she played like a demon. Normally, she was simply a "pretty good" player, but that day, she scrambled and stretched and spun like she'd been born to the game. She won the first game easily, 40–love.

But Dee was no slouch when it came to tennis. Growing up in Southern California, she'd been able to play any time she felt like it, just by walking across the street to a neighbor's court. She won the second game, 40–20.

"You're getting good, Toby!" Dee called across the net. "But the third game will show just *how* good. Ready?"

"I've been ready for five minutes," Toby

called back. "Quit stalling and let's play!"

Dee loved competition, but she really wasn't out to prove anything. And if she lost, well, she'd win another time. No big deal.

But Toby did want to prove something, even though she wasn't sure what it was. All she knew was that it had suddenly become very important for her to win the last game. Dee was having fun. Toby was out for blood.

In a very short time, the score was 30–20, Toby, and it was Toby's serve. Her serve was still one of her weakest points, but today, she'd already gotten two aces. Her eyes like bright green slits, she wiped her forehead with her arm, then bounced the ball a couple of times, trying to steady herself. If she could ace Dee now, she'd have it won.

Just as Toby was about to toss the ball into the air, she heard a familiar rattling sound on the road behind the courts. Ignore it, she told herself, realizing what it was. But the rattle got louder and Toby couldn't ignore it. Turning, she saw Randy's pick-up bouncing down the road, every loose screw and bolt jangling like crazy.

"Come on, Toby!" Dee yelled. "I've got to get to English!"

But even though she wanted to, Toby couldn't turn back. Princess Allegra was sitting next to Randy, in the same seat Toby had ridden in so many times. Toby caught a glimpse of her long, dark hair swirling in the wind and then, as the truck rounded a bend, Randy caught a glimpse of Toby.

With a big grin and a toot of the horn, Randy leaned his head out and hollered, "Way to go, Texas!"

Toby didn't get her ace, and Dee won the third game.

"Well, what do you think?" Andy asked, her breath coming in little gasps. "Do I have a chance?"

"If you don't, nobody does," Matt said. "That last run-through was beautiful."

"You didn't think it was too fast? I know I sometimes rush my steps, and when I'm nervous, I rush even more. And you can bet I'll be nervous at the audition," Andy went on. "I mean, it's my one and only chance, and I don't want to blow it. So if there was anything wrong, tell me now."

Matt laughed and held up his hands to stop the flow of words. "Help!" he said.

"Right, that's another one of my problems," Andy said. "I talk too much. Will you come to the audition, and if I so much as open my mouth, will you promise to put a Band-Aid on it?"

"I'll try to come, but I can't promise," Matt told her. "I go to school, too, remember? But you don't need a Band-Aid, and you won't need me. Just do what you did today and everything will be fine."

"You don't really know that for sure," Andy said. "You're just being optimistic."

"Sure I am. Why be anything else?" Laughing again, Matt took her hand. "Come on. Watching you dance made me tired. But some food will perk me up, so let's eat."

As Andy and Matt walked toward the Greaf Diner for a late breakfast – early lunch, Jane was just finishing her last blueberry pancake. "Wonderful," she said, scraping up the syrup with her fork. "They serve these at Canby Hall, you know, but they put rubber in the pancake batter and instead of blueberries, they use bullets."

"Ah-ha, the old blue bullet trick," Cary joked. He actually was wearing a red rose, stuck in a buttonhole of his denim vest, and as he filled the sugar bowls along the counter, he glanced at Jane's empty plate and laughed. "May I interest you in another stack of those taste treats?"

"I'm always interested in more food," Jane admitted with a laugh. "But I have a bad habit of falling asleep when my stomach's too full. And I have a history teacher this afternoon who frowns on students sleeping in her classroom. So, I'd better not." Licking the last of the syrup from her fork, Jane pushed her plate aside and took a sip of coffee. "Okay, I'm awake," she said. "Now tell me what you want my advice about."

Cary nodded. "Her royal highness was in here yesterday with her most devoted follower, the honorable Randy Crowell. We got to talking, and guess what?" His blue eyes twinkled mischievously.

"What?"

"It turns out that Princess Allegra loves rock music, almost as much as I do. And when I told her that I'm part of a band, and even do a little composing myself, well, you can imagine her excitement."

"All right!" Jane was blushing. "I was wrong about her. She turned out to have some tastes I didn't think she'd have. I knew you wouldn't let me forget that comment I made, about how she might not like a group like Ambulance." Laughing at the grin on Cary's face, she said, "Now that you've paid me back for insulting you, what do you want my advice about?"

"Wait," Cary said. "Andy just came in with Matt. I'd like her opinion, too."

After Matt and Andy had ordered, Cary told them that Princess Allegra had asked to hear Ambulance play. "She said she'd never heard a rock group live, and she knew we were all busy getting ready for finals, but if we could spare a little time, she'd treasure the memory for the rest of her life." He sighed. "Naturally, I couldn't refuse."

"Naturally," Andy said dryly.

"I talked to the other guys and they're willing," Cary went on. "So the question is, do we make it a private performance for the princess, or do we invite lots of kids and have a big bash? Sort of a prefinals blowout?"

"I don't think Allegra would have half as much fun if it was just a private performance," Andy said. "Besides, it would seem kind of snobby, and she's not like that. I vote for a party."

The others agreed. "Let's make it Saturday night," Jane suggested. "Nobody does much studying then anyway, and it's her last night. We can make it a bon voyage party."

"Saturday night it is," Cary said. "I'll round up some guys from Oakley, and you take care of the invitations at Canby Hall. Oh," he went on, "be sure to tell Toby. I saw her walking around town this morning and she was as pale as a ghost. My diagnosis is too much studying, and a party's the best medicine for that."

Jane and Andy exchanged glances. It was hard enough to talk Toby into going to any crowded party, let alone a going-away party for Princess Allegra.

"She won't come," Jane said, as the two of them walked back to Baker House. "She won't even bother to say no, either. She just won't show up."

"Maybe," Andy said. "But who knows? She's probably so happy Allegra's leaving, she might come just so she can be the first one to say good-bye. Of course, she'll mean 'good riddance.' "

Jane smiled and then said thoughtfully, "I can't help wondering what's going to happen when Allegra does leave."

"What do you mean?"

"Well, does Toby expect things to go back to the way they were?" Jane asked. "Because they won't. Things have already changed, and it's too late to change them back."

CHAPTER TWELVE

After her last class, Jane hurried back to the dorm, hoping to catch Toby in one of her rare appearances in 407. Andy had had the same idea, and when the two of them met in front of Baker House, they agreed that they weren't going to let Toby give them the silent treatment this time.

First they went to check their mail. Jane had a letter from her sister, Charlotte, and for Andy, there was another box from Chicago.

"I wonder what it is this time," Jane said, trying not to sound too eager and failing completely.

Andy held the box in one hand, testing its weight. Then she sniffed it and smiled. "I thought so. Here, smell it."

Jane sniffed. "Gingerbread?"

"The best. Here," Andy said, handing her the box. "I'm putting you in charge of it.

Save me some, but don't let me touch it till the audition's over. I've eaten too much junk this week already, and if I start in on that, I won't be able to leap two inches off the ground."

As they started up the stairs, they almost collided with Meredith, who was coming down at twice her usual speed, which was fast to begin with. "Sorry," she said. Then the distracted frown disappeared from her face. "Oh, good. You're just the two I wanted to see. I'd like to see Toby, too, but I can't find her. Now that I think of it, I almost never see Toby these days."

"Oh, she's around someplace," Andy said. "Probably outside. You know Toby, she needs her daily quota of fresh air."

"Mmm." Meredith looked at them thoughtfully. Well, at least you're here. Come on up to my room, why don't you?"

It was obvious that whatever Meredith wanted to say, she wanted to say in private. Which made it important. Hoping it was wonderfully important and not terribly important, Jane and Andy followed their housemother up to her big comfortable room on the fifth floor.

Once inside, Meredith poured three glasses of orange juice, took a sip of hers, and then came right to the point. "About an hour ago, I had a call from Ms. Allardyce."

"Uh-oh," Andy said under her breath.

"No, it wasn't like that," Meredith laughed.

"She was just puzzled, she said, as to why Princess Allegra had been so downcast at tea today. It was such a change, she said, from the bubbling, laughing girl she'd seen three days ago, and she wondered if I knew the reason for the change."

"What did you tell her?" Jane asked.

"I told her that I had no idea, that the last time I'd seen the princess, she seemed on top of the world. But then," Meredith went on, "after I'd spoken to Ms. Allardyce, I decided to drop in on Allegra, just to see if everything was all right. I haven't seen much of her lately, either. I found her crying in her room, looking like her last ship had just sunk." Meredith finished her juice and leaned back in her chair. "So I thought I'd ask if you knew what the trouble is."

"Well . . ." Andy said.

"Well . . ." Jane echoed.

Meredith smiled. "I get it. You know, but you're afraid to tell me because Allegra doesn't want you to, or you think she wouldn't want you to."

"That's about it," Andy said.

"Okay, I understand." Meredith thought for a second, and then stood up. "Listen, I don't want to know all the details. I wouldn't even ask if I didn't think it was important. Ms. Allardyce is concerned because Allegra's a princess. I'm concerned because, for as long as she's here, Allegra's one of my girls."

"That makes her lucky," Andy said with a grin.

"I agree." Jane nodded briskly in one of her classic gestures of approval. Then she turned to Andy. "I think Allegra should come talk to Merry, don't you?"

"Definitely," Andy said.

Merry laughed, delighted. "Thanks for the vote of confidence. Really. But I tried to talk to her already and didn't get anywhere. That's okay — we hardly know each other. But *you* know her."

"Yes, but . . ."

"Like I said, I don't want all the details." Merry told them. "You don't have to tell me if she had a fight with Randy Corwell, or if she's homesick, or even if she found a pea under her mattress. All I really want to know is should I keep trying to talk to her? Will whatever's going on get worse? Or should I just leave it alone?"

Jane and Andy looked at each other, and without words, they knew they were thinking the same thing.

"I think," Andy said, "that you should just let it ride. I won't kid you — Allegra's unhappy. You saw that for yourself. But it can't get any worse than it is now."

When Andy and Jane walked down the stairs from Meredith's room, they found Allegra waiting for them on the fourth-floor landing.

"I'm sorry!" she said at once. "I saw you coming up here with her, and I just knew she was going to quiz you about me. But there was nothing I could do to stop it — she'd already seen me crying like a baby. I'm afraid I wasn't very convincing when I told her that nothing was wrong."

"Why did you tell her that?" Jane asked. "Something is wrong, and it's nothing to be ashamed about."

"Right," Andy said, as the three of them walked slowly down the hall. "You know, you ought to talk to Merry. She's okay — she's more than okay — and she might be able to help."

Allegra shook her head. "I know she's okay, but I couldn't possibly talk to her about this. Anyway, what would she do? Tell my family that in her opinion, I shouldn't have to marry Frederick because I'm in love with Randy?" She gave a crooked little smile. "A hundred people could tell them that, and it wouldn't matter a bit. My future's all set. Unless it's discovered that Prince Frederick is a thief, or a murderer, or some other kind of unsavory character, I'm trapped."

"So what are you saying?" Andy asked. "That you're giving up?"

"No, the trap hasn't been sprung yet," Allegra said. "I've still got a little time to think of a way to avoid it. I'm sure I'll come up with something. But I have to do it on my own — talking with Meredith would be a waste of time right now."

Just as Andy was about to argue, doors began to open along the hallway and girls emerged, heading for the dining hall to see if there was anything edible for dinner. Jane quickly put the package of gingerbread in 407 and then joined Andy and Allegra at the end of the hall. As the three of them walked toward the stairs, she told Allegra about Saturday's party and Ambulance.

Allegra's eyes got very shiny all of a sudden. "It's a going-away party, isn't it?"

"Well, sort of," Andy said, "but if you're going to cry the second the band starts playing, then we'll call it something else."

"How about farewell?" Jane suggested. "Or au revoir? Those don't seem quite as final."

"No," Allegra said firmly. "Let's not play games with words. I'm going away and that's that."

When the sound of the last footstep had died away, the door of the fourth-floor broom closet slowly opened. One cowboy-booted foot emerged, followed by a second. Finally, Toby scooted all the way out and gingerly stretched her cramped muscles.

The broom closet was about the only place on the floor where a person could get any privacy, and Toby had gone there to avoid Jane and Andy. Trying to avoid her two best friends made her feel slightly sick, but she

just couldn't face their questions right now.
All they wanted was to talk, and all she wanted
was silence.

She'd only meant to stay there for a few
minutes — her long legs could only take it
in small doses. And she hadn't meant to eaves-
drop on anybody's conversation, but once she
heard Jane and Andy and the princess, she
was stuck.

So Princess Allegra was upset about having
to go home, and even more upset that she had
to marry that prince. Toby didn't blame her
— it sounded like she'd gotten the bad end
of a bargain. But Toby couldn't feel any
sympathy for her. She'd come over here,
played around with people's feelings, and
made a mess out of everything. As far as Toby
was concerned, the sooner she left, the better.

Toby touched her toes a couple of times,
then went into 407 and ate a Peanut Butter
Cup and an apple, trying not to think about
it anymore. Not only did she not want to talk
about it, she didn't even want it to enter her
mind. In her opinion, the entire subject was
better off buried and forgotten. As if she
could shut off her thoughts, Toby closed her
eyes tightly, rolled up in her blanket, and
fell asleep.

The next thing she knew, a finger was
poking her in the shoulder. "What," she said,
her voice muffled by the heavy blanket.

"October Houston, you unroll yourself
from that moth-eaten horse blanket right this

minute. I've got something to say, and I'm not about to say it to a lump on a bed!"

Toby uncovered her face and stared up at Andy, whose eyes were snapping with anger.

"Besides," Andy went on, "it's spring outside. It's warm. It makes me sweat just to look at you!"

With a half smile, Toby got rid of the blanket. "There," she said. "Are you cooler now?"

"Much." Andy, never at a loss for words, took a deep breath and started. "Listen, I know you've been feeling rotten ever since Allegra and Randy got together. I know it seems really unfair that somebody could just appear out of the blue like that and change everything. What I want to know is when you're going to stop sulking and do something about it!"

At that moment, Jane came in, sensed the mood in the room, and did an about-face.

"No, come on in," Andy insisted, waving her back. "You're part of this team, too."

Almost tiptoeing, Jane moved to her side of the room as quickly as possible. Andy waited until she was sitting at her desk and then turned back to Toby. "You won't talk to us, and that's fine. You won't talk to Merry, and that's fine, too. You seem to think you can solve it yourself. Great! Except I don't see any solving going on. All I see is a bunch of sulking."

Feeling like she had to move or burst, Andy

placed the fingertips of one hand against the wall and did some pliés. The room was quiet.

Jane shifted uncomfortably in her chair. Outbursts of emotion were frowned upon in Louisburg Square, and she didn't think she'd ever get used to them. Andy was different — her highs and lows were so intense, she couldn't keep them inside. She was upset and frustrated, and even though Jane had the urge to leave, she knew she owed it to Toby, and to Andy, to stay and be part of the "team." Before she could think of what to say, though, Toby spoke up.

"Sorry," she mumbled. "I know I've been about as much fun as a brush fire."

Her knees bent, her back straight, Andy said, "Brush fires are like a day at the circus compared to the way you've been acting." But she smiled when she said it, and some of the tension went out of the room.

"Sorry," Toby said again. "I wish things were different. I wish the princess had never come. But don't worry — the old Toby'll be back in no time."

"That's good to hear," Jane said. "But how are you going to accomplish that?"

"Just sit tight and wait."

"Wait?"

Toby nodded. "The princess leaves on Sunday."

Andy looked confused. "So?"

"So she'll be gone," Toby said simply. "And then things'll be back to normal."

Andy stopped bobbing up and down and stared at her. "Maybe you're right. But the only person you've been talking about is Allegra," she said quietly. "It seems to me you've forgotten that there's somebody else involved."

"Who?"

"Randy." Gathering up her shower cap and towel, Andy started for the door. "If he starts acting like nothing's happened after Allegra leaves, then that would mean he didn't care much about her. Do you really think he doesn't?"

CHAPTER THIRTEEN

Saturday morning arrived with a strong breeze that sent patches of grey-white clouds scuttling across the blue skies and bent the tulips in the carefully tended flower beds of Canby Hall.

"I hope it doesn't rain," Jane said, looking out the window. "At least not until I get back from town."

Andy put her ballet slippers and a towel into her canvas bag and zipped it up. "What are you going into town for?"

"I need some new yellow marking pens," Jane said, pulling on a pair of jeans and a pale blue LaCoste shirt. "And don't laugh."

To hide her grin, Andy tugged a pink, short-sleeved sweatshirt over her head. "You're going to keep that stationery store in business, that's for sure. I bet they love it when they see you coming. 'Great!' they say, 'it's the magic marker monster! The cash register will be full today!' "

"Very funny," Jane said, smiling slightly. "However, no amount of joking will stop me from highlighting. I refuse to give it up."

Andy fluffed her hair with her fingers and laughed. "Hey, if it gets you on the honor roll, that's what counts. Besides, I don't want you to stop. Then I couldn't tease you about it."

"Oh, well, I wouldn't want to spoil your fun," Jane said dryly.

Just then, Maggie and Dee stopped by, also on their way to town, so the four girls left Baker House together.

"Dee and I were talking," Maggie said as they walked along. "And we thought since this is Allegra's last day here, maybe we should buy her a going-away present and give it to her at the party tonight."

Dee laughed. "I still can't believe it," she said. "I was so sure the princess was going to be a real snob, walking around with her nose in the air. And it turns out I really like her."

"I was kind of down on her, too, at first," Andy admitted. "But I'm going to miss her. It was fun having her here."

"Everybody felt that way after the first couple of days," Jane said. "Almost everybody," she added, thinking of Toby.

"Well, she's not gone yet," Maggie reminded them. "What about the present?

Everybody else we've talked to thinks it's a good idea. What about you? Do you want to go in on it?"

Andy and Jane didn't answer right away. Both of them were wondering what Toby would think. Would she be hurt? Would she be angry? Would she think they didn't care about her feelings? Of course, she knew they had to spend time with Allegra — they were her hostesses. But she also knew that they'd gone from being hostesses to being friends, and they weren't sure how she felt about that.

"What's the problem?" Dee asked, after about thirty seconds of silence had gone by. "This is not a decision that's going to change the course of the world, you know."

"If you're short of money," Maggie said helpfully, "I'll be glad to chip in. You can pay me back later."

"It's not money," Jane said. Reaching into her purse, she pulled out her soft leather billfold and took out some money. "Allegra's our friend. Of course, I'll contribute."

"So will I," Andy said, rummaging in her bag. She pulled out a dollar bill and some change and gave it to Maggie. Looking at Jane, she gave her a warm smile of approval. "Jane's right. Allegra's our friend, and when a friend goes away, you give her a gift."

Both of them were glad they'd done it. Toby meant a lot to them, but there was room in their lives for many friends, and Allegra was one of them.

After the other three split off in the direction of Greenleaf's main street, Andy hurried to the auditorium. Matt had told her it would be empty for about half an hour, and she'd jumped at the chance. It was important, she thought, to rehearse as many times as she could on the stage, because that's where she'd be doing the audition.

Matt couldn't make it, but he'd told her where the main light switch was, and after turning it on, Andy went on stage and did a few warm-up exercises. Then she switched on the tape. Coming from such a small speaker, the music was tinny and weak, but Andy didn't notice. In her mind, there was a complete orchestra in the pit, the auditorium was crowded with a hushed audience, and the stage was hers to fill.

And she did fill it, twirling and leaping from one side to the other, moving through the air as if she were immune to gravity. When she finished, she knew she'd never been as good in her life. It was the most exhilarating experience she'd ever had, and after holding her final pose for a few seconds, she sat down on the stage and laughed out loud.

Finally, she got to her feet, switched off the tape recorder, and left the stage. As she was walking up the aisle, she saw someone standing just inside the doors. "Hi," she said. "I hope I didn't keep you waiting. I'm finished now, so the stage is all yours."

"Thank you, Ms. Cord," someone said,

and Andy immediately recognized the voice of Adele Brinco, the woman who would be teaching the class in advanced dance.

"Oh. Ms. Brinco." Andy stopped in front of the teacher, a short, wiry woman with high cheekbones and piercing pale-gray eyes. "I'm sorry. I didn't know you were waiting for the stage."

"I wasn't," Ms. Brinco said. "I just happened to be passing by." She looked at Andy for a moment. "Was that the routine you'll be doing for the audition, Ms. Cord?"

"Umm . . ." Andy wasn't sure what to say. What if the lady had hated it? Well, it was too late to do anything about that now. Besides, it was good, she knew it was. "Yes," she said.

Ms. Brinco lifted her chin and peered up at Andy. "A word of advice, Ms. Cord."

Andy steeled herself for a barrage of criticism. "Yes?"

"Don't change a thing."

As Matt listened to Andy tell the story, his handsome face broke into a big smile. "That means you've made it!"

"Well, not quite," Andy said. "I have to be as good at the audition as I was today, and that won't be easy." Then she laughed excitedly. "But I bet I can do it!"

"Sure you can." Matt took her hand, and together, they walked into Oakley Prep's gym to help get it ready for the party.

Using a combination of charm, quick wit, and fast talking, Cary had managed to convince his school to let them use the gym that night. The headmaster had been reluctant, but when Cary started talking about saving international relations, he told Jane, the man had given in gracefully.

"What did he think would happen?" Jane asked. "Was he afraid Montavia would attack America?"

"No, he's too smart for that," Cary admitted. "I think he just wanted to get rid of me, and giving in was the easiest way. Anyway, the gym's ours."

Jane looked around. At least thirty Canby Hall girls were there, along with as many Oakley Prep boys, and they'd all volunteered to help decorate the gym. It was nice of them, Jane thought, except it was such a spur-of-the-moment party that no one had had the time to make or buy new decorations, so they'd brought leftovers. Red, green, orange, black, and pink crepe paper streamers were strung from the ceiling. Cardboard pumpkins lined the walls, along with Frosty the Snowman and Santa Claus faces, plus a few Easter bunnies and some large posters of rock stars.

"This is a combination of Christmas, Halloween, and Easter," Jane said. "With a little heavy metal thrown in." She sighed. "I wish we'd had more time. It could have been lovely."

"Don't worry about it," Cary laughed. "Nobody pays any attention to it anyway, not after the band starts playing."

Cary went back to tuning his guitar, and after a few minutes of ear-splitting sounds that set Jane's teeth on edge, the band came together in a spontaneous jam session. Someone would play a series of notes, and the rest would jump in as if they'd been rehearsing all day. They didn't sing, but they laughed a lot, sometimes calling out jokes to each other without missing a beat. They played for about half an hour, the music bouncing around the gym like a warm, playful wind, lifting everyone's spirits with it.

"This is going to be one great party!" Cary shouted when they finished. And Jane, always amazed that a band calling itself "Ambulance" could acttually produce music, had to agree.

The wind outside the gym was warm, too, but as everyone discovered when they left for dinner, it wasn't very playful. It was dead serious. As Jane and Andy hurried back to Baker House to eat and then change, they felt the first fat drops of rain splash on their heads. By the time they left the dorm again, on the way back to Oakley Prep, they needed raincoats and umbrellas.

"This is not the way to arrive at a party," Jane said, sidestepping a puddle. The wind, stronger than ever, turned her umbrella inside out, and her hair was immediately plastered to her head. "I'm going to look like a drowned rat."

"I tried to tell you," Andy said. She was wearing a yellow hooded rain slicker that came down to her knees and matching yellow boots that came halfway up her legs. "I have an extra one of these; I don't know why you wouldn't take it."

"I've always hated foul weather gear," Jane said, struggling with her umbrella. "Even on sailboats. It makes me feel like I'm in a steam bath."

"Speaking of foul weather," Andy said. "Did you see Toby today?"

"No." Jane sidestepped another puddle. "I didn't see her at all. She must have spent the day at the library."

"I saw her at the tennis courts, looking for somebody to play with," Andy said. "I know she can play the game, but today she looked completely out of place there. She looked lost." Andy peered out at Jane from under her hood. "You know, we were saying today how we'd miss Allegra?"

"Yes."

"Well, Toby isn't even gone. But I miss her."

"I do, too." Jane sighed. "After tonight, after Allegra's gone, we'll get Toby back. Somehow."

Once they entered the brightly lit gym, the girls tried to shed their worries along with their raincoats. Everyone else was having such a good time, it was almost impossible not to join in.

Andy started dancing almost the minute she entered, first with Matt, and then with at least a dozen other boys. She wanted to be a ballet dancer, but she could move to any kind of music. As long as the band kept playing, Andy kept dancing.

Jane danced a few times, but mostly she walked around, keeping one eye on the gym doors for Randy and Allegra. They should be here soon, she thought, checking her watch. Allegra had said they were going to have one farewell cheeseburger at The Greaf together, and then they'd get to the party at about seven-thirty. It was seven forty-five already, according to Jane's watch. Well, maybe they'd ordered double cheeseburgers.

By eight-fifteen, just as everyone was starting to wonder where the guest of honor was, Randy came bursting through the gym doors. "They're here!" somebody shouted. The band stopped in mid-song so the drummer could play a drum roll, and everyone began to clap.

Ignoring the applause, Randy hurried through the crowd to Jane and Andy, his eyes slightly wild and his face white. When he reached them, he gripped Jane's shoulder. "Is she here?" he asked, breathing fast and hard. "Is Allegra here?"

"No," Jane told him in surprise. "She's with you, isn't she?"

Randy shook his head, frantically running his fingers through his hair.

"Well, where is she?" Andy asked.

By this time, the crowd had realized that something was happening, and they stopped clapping as the last of the drum roll died away. In the silence that followed, two men hurried into the gym, shouldering the party-goers aside as they strode quickly over to Randy, Jane, and Andy. The two men were Joseph and Rodger, Allegra's bodyguards.

"Where is she?" one of them asked. He spoke quietly, but no one missed the tension in his voice. Allegra had disappeared again, but this time, everyone could tell it wasn't a game.

CHAPTER FOURTEEN

I'm telling you, I don't know what happened!" Randy said again. "Allegra and I were going to meet at The Greaf because I was already in town, and it was faster just to meet there."

One of the bodyguards nodded. "She got there at 6:30," he said. "She took a booth, then went through the door that leads to the restrooms. She wasn't back when you came, and when we got permission to search, we found that there's a side door out of the place. That must be how she left."

"Yes, but I was as surprised as you were." Randy shoved his hands in his pockets and glared at the two bodyguards. "I know we've pulled a few tricks before, but not this time."

It was almost nine o'clock. The party had broken up quickly, and most people rushed through the pouring rain back to their dorms. But Jane, Andy, Joseph, Rodger, and Randy had gone to Ms. Allardyce's house. The headmistress, notified by now that the princess was missing, had called a meeting to find out exactly what had happened. Meredith was there, too, and so was Toby.

"I don't understand," Ms. Allardyce said to Randy now. "What 'tricks' are you talking about?"

One of the bodyguards answered first. "He and the princess would sneak away so they could be alone for a little while," he told her. "The princess always told someone where she'd be, and we always found her. But this time, it's not working out that way."

"Because it wasn't a trick this time," Randy said, looking tired and upset. "I don't understand why you won't believe me. Allegra and I . . . well, she means a lot to me."

Toby, her face reddening, kept her eyes on her hands.

Ms. Allardyce looked at Randy for a moment. Then she cleared her throat. "I know the Crowell family quite well," she told the bodyguards. "If Mr. Crowell says he and the princess weren't playing a trick on you, then they weren't." She stood up from behind her desk. "The question is what do we do now?"

"Are you sure you don't have any idea where she might be?" Meredith asked the girls of 407.

Jane was silent, thinking; Toby sat still as a statue. Finally, Andy spoke up. "She was

upset about having to go home tomorrow,"
she said. "Maybe she decided to take a walk
to kind of calm down."

"In the rain?" Ms. Allardyce asked.

"Well, I do it all the time," Andy told her.
"Rain or shine, if I'm upset, a walk always
helps."

"She'd be back by now," one of the bodyguards pointed out.

"Maybe she got lost," Andy said, realizing
how silly it sounded. Who could get lost in
Greenleaf?

"Could she be in her room?" Jane asked
suddenly. "She might have come back here
just to be alone. Did anyone check her room?"

"That's the first place I looked," Meredith
told her. "As of twenty minutes ago, it was
empty. So was 407."

More silence, while everyone tried to think
where Allegra might be.

Finally, Ms. Allardyce cleared her throat
again. She was calm but pale as she said, "The
princess might have decided to go for a walk,
it's true. But I'm afraid we must consider all
the possibilities."

"Kidnapping," one of the bodyguards said
immediately.

Toby's face was still unreadable, but Jane
and Andy were truly shocked—they hadn't
even thought Allegra might be kidnapped.
Greenleaf was such a quiet, peaceful little
town. Not that it didn't have its share of
problems, but kidnapping just seemed com-

pletely out of place in a town where three parking tickets and a broken-into vending machine were a big day for the police. Could Greenleaf, Massachusetts really be the site of a kidnapping?

Most of the others seemed to think so. Ms. Allardyce was already on the phone to the police, and the bodyguards were instructing Meredith on what to do if she got a ransom note or a phone call. Watching them in action started to make it seem real.

"Very well," Ms. Allardyce said, hanging up the phone. "The police are sending men out to search the area, and I will notify the F.B.I. when and if we're able to confirm that it is a kidnapping." She stared at the others for a moment, still pale, but still in control. "In the meantime, I suggest we all go about our business and try to remain calm. You three are excused," she said, nodding to Jane, Andy, and Toby. "And Meredith, I think you'd better inform the rest of the girls. I hate to alarm them, but it's important that they know what to do in case the call comes in to one of their rooms."

Meredith nodded, and she and the girls from 407 began to leave. As they were going out the door, they heard Randy inform one of the bodyguards in no uncertain terms that he was going to voluteer his services to the police.

"She's as important to me as she is to you," he said. "Maybe more."

Hearing him, Toby hunched her shoulders and ducked her chin deep into her rain poncho, as if trying to shut the words out.

It was still raining, and Meredith, Jane, and Andy walked quickly, hurrying back to the warmth and comfort of Baker House. Toby trailed behind, her head down.

"Whew!" Andy said, as they sloshed along. "I feel like this just isn't real. It doesn't seem like it could happen here."

"That's what I thought at first," Jane said. "But then I realized that if there was a kidnapping, it doesn't have anything to do with where, it has to do with who."

"In this case, a princess," Meredith said. "A wealthy princess, and an only child. Jane's right — when you think about who she is, it starts to seem real."

"And everyone knew she was here," Jane went on. "The Greenleaf paper did an entire page on it, and my mother even sent me a clipping about her from one of the Boston papers."

"I'm beginning to get it," Andy said. "She was big news. People with kidnapping on their minds knew exactly where to find her. Whew!" she said again. "That makes me shiver!"

"We don't know for certain that it is a kidnapping yet," Meredith reminded them. "So don't let your imaginations run away with you. Remember," she said with a smile, "I'm counting on you to set an example for everybody else — and the Canby Hall girl never comes unglued in the face of adversity."

"What does she do?" Andy asked.

"She makes herself a cup of coffee or cocoa, she forces herself to relax, and then she thinks things through." Merry smiled again. "Once the adversity has passed, *then* she comes unglued."

Many cups of coffee and cocoa were brewed that night in Baker House, as the residents gathered in their rooms to discuss what might have happened to Princess Allegra. Everyone was worried, many were frightened, a few had trouble sleeping. But no one came unglued.

Meredith had called a special meeting in the dining room and told most of the residents what had happened. Not everyone was there, since it was Saturday night and not yet sign-in time, but their roommates promised to pass the word. After the meeting, Room 407 was filled almost to overflowing. Since Jane and Andy were such good friends with the princess, a lot of girls thought they might know more about the situation than anyone else. They didn't, but that didn't stop the crowds from coming.

"Maybe we should put a sign on our door," Andy said at one point. "Something like, 'We're as ignorant as you are.'"

"That won't work," Dee told her. "What everybody really wants is to just talk. That's

why I came in. Talking makes it not so scary."
She leaned back on Toby's bed, and then
suddenly sat up again. "How does she stand
this thing?" she asked, running her hands
across Toby's blanket. "It's about as cozy as
a Brillo pad."

Without thinking, Jane said, "One girl's
Brillo pad is another girl's comforter."

For the first time in two hours, Andy
laughed. "That really says it!" she told Jane.
"That scratchy old blanket gives Toby a lot
of comfort."

"I don't see how," Dee remarked, getting
off the bed. "But anyway, where is Toby? Did
she join the search or something?"

"I, uh, I don't think so," Jane said quickly.
"She's probably down in the study room."

"Right," Andy said. "You know Toby —
she's turning into a regular bookworm these
days."

Neither of them knew where Toby was.

"Well, I hope she's somewhere in the
dorm," Dee said seriously.

"Oh, come on, Dee," Andy said. "I know
Toby's not poor, but I don't think she's kidnap
material."

"I wasn't thinking of that," Dee said. "I
was just thinking that it's almost sign-in time.
So if Toby's out riding the purple sage, she'd
better hurry."

Since there was no purple sage in the entire
state of Massachusetts, Toby wasn't out riding
it, but she wasn't in the study room, either.

And she definitely wasn't hurrying to get back to Baker House before sign-in time.

As Jane and Andy and Merry had hurried toward the dorm from Ms. Allardyce's house, Toby had kept falling farther and farther behind. And when they got to Baker House, Toby had quickly decided not to go in yet. Everyone in the entire building was going to be talking about the same thing — Princess Allegra. And the princess was not Toby's favorite subject. So Toby just tied the hood of her poncho a little tighter and set off on a walk in the rain. By the time she came back, she thought, maybe most of the talk would have died down, and she wouldn't have to listen to it.

The walk helped her escape from the talk about the kidnapping, but it couldn't stop her thinking about it. And what Toby thought was that Princess Allegra hadn't been kidnapped at all. Not for a minute. In Toby's opinion, the princess had decided to run away.

It made sense. Princess Allegra was all in an uproar because she had to go home and marry that duke, or whatever he was. She might not get to come back to Canby Hall, and she might not ever see Randy again. She couldn't see any way out of the mess and so what did she do? She ran.

Toby walked on, the heels of her boots sinking a little in the spongy grass. Didn't the princess know the mess was just going to keep on following her? Probably not. She probably didn't even think about it. She just saw a way out, and it looked easy, so she took it.

It wasn't easy, though. Toby knew because she'd tried it once, the time she'd decided that Canby Hall and her two rotten roommates just weren't her cup of tea. Fortunately, her two rotten roommates turned out to be two good friends, and they'd stopped her. But Toby understood how the princess felt. When things were messy, you sometimes just wanted to run.

Of course, Toby thought, she'd had a place to run to — her home in Texas. The princess didn't have anyplace, which made it even more of a dumb fool thing to do.

Suddenly, a pair of headlights gleamed from behind her, and somebody honked a horn. Turning, Toby saw Randy's pick-up pulling over to the side of the road. Randy rolled down the passenger window and stuck his head out. "I thought that was you," he called. "Need a ride?"

Toby wiped the raindrops off her nose and ran over to the window. "No, thanks," she said. "I just felt like a walk."

Randy managed a smile. "I guess you don't get rain like this in your part of Texas."

"Nope," Toby said. "And we sure could use a little of it once in a while."

He nodded, then sighed. "Well, if you don't want to ride, I think I'll drive on. The police wouldn't let me help with the search, and the bodyguards are convinced it's a kidnapping and think the search is a waste of time. So there's nothing left to do right now but wait."

Toby couldn't think of what to say at first, but then she took a good look at his face and realized he was more upset than he sounded. "I'm sorry this happened," she told him.

He nodded again. "Thanks, Texas. Well, I'm off." He shifted gears and started to pull away, then braked again. "I almost forgot to ask," he called out. "Did you hear anything more about Max?"

Toby blinked, surprised that he'd even think of it right now. "He's fine," she told him. "My dad meant my Uncle Max. He just forgot to mention it."

Randy chuckled, shaking his head. "Well, I'm glad to hear it," he said. "Even though I've never met your horse, I feel like I know him."

After Randy drove on, Toby kept walking, smiling to herself. Randy must have been feeling just about as rotten as could be, she thought, but even with all that's on his mind, he asked her about Max. That was Randy for you. He'd been like that since she first met him, and he hadn't changed a bit.

Without really meaning to, Toby had walked into Greenleaf. It must be just about sign-in time, she thought. She could just make it back if she started now.

Instead, Toby kept on walking. If they were going to call off the search, then she'd better find the princess before she actually did run away. Not that Toby cared that much about the princess, she told herself, but plenty of other people did care. And some of those other people meant a lot to Toby. Besides, letting the princess run off in a strange country was like sending somebody across the plain without water — your conscience just wouldn't let you do it.

There were two ways to leave town if you didn't have a car — by train or by bus. Toby came to the bus station first, which was squeezed in between a pharmacy and a hardware store. The two stores were closed up and dark, but a faint light was shining in the waiting room of the bus station. Toby walked up and peered through the grimy window.

A man, probably the ticket-taker, was sitting behind a little window with a grill on it, his head buried in a paperback book. Off to the side, out of his sight and wearing a wrinkled tan raincoat and black plastic rain hat, sat Princess Allegra.

CHAPTER FIFTEEN

Toby pulled open the door, which screeched on its hinges, but the man behind the counter didn't even lift his eyes from the pages of his book. Pushing her hood back, Toby walked directly over to the princess, who sat up straight and slowly took the plastic rain hat off her head.

"I suppose it's just a matter of time now, isn't it, before everyone else comes?" the princess asked.

"Everyone else?" Toby frowned. "Oh, you think I've brought the posse, I guess." She shook her head. "Nope. It's just me."

Allerga relaxed a little. "Then you didn't come to stop me?"

"I just came to find you," Toby said. "I had a hunch you'd decided to take off, and I wanted to see if I was right." As she talked, a puddle of rainwater was slowly forming at her feet. Finally, she slipped the poncho over her head, showering Allegra with drops of water. "Everybody else thinks you've been kidnapped, you know."

Allegra nodded. "I saw the police cars, and I knew Joseph and Rodger must have jumped to that conclusion," she said. "They're always fretting about kidnappers."

"How come the police didn't see you here?" Toby asked.

"Because I walked around a long time, and I saw them first. So I just waited until they'd left here." She leaned forward and glanced at the ticket man. "He didn't even look at me when I came in," she said. "I think the President of the United States could arrive and that man wouldn't stop reading. It must be the most fascinating book ever written."

Tired of standing, Toby sat on the bench across from Allegra and stretched her legs out. "Everybody's real worried about you," she said, thinking especially of Randy.

Allegra lowered her eyes, looking ashamed. "I didn't want to frighten people. I'm going to write some letters just as soon as I get to . . . to wherever I'm going."

Toby nodded. "That sounds like a good idea. Where *are* you going?"

Allegra almost laughed. "I've no idea," she admitted. "I know that sounds foolish, but I didn't plan this at all. It just occurred to me about half an hour before I was supposed to meet Randy. And it seemed like the only way out." She looked down and tried to smooth some of the wrinkles out of the raincoat. It was about two sizes too large, and the black plastic rain hat was one of the ugliest things Toby had ever seen. "I found these in the lost and found bin in Baker House," she said. "They looked as if they'd been there for years. Once I'd decided to go, I thought I should have some sort of disguise."

Toby put her head to one side and studied Allegra, who managed to look graceful even on the hard, uncomfortable bench. Toby herself had slumped down until she was almost sitting on her tailbone, but Allegra's back was straight as an arrow. "I don't think the disguise works," she said after a minute. "You could wear rags and you'd still look like a princess. You carry yourself like a thoroughbred. You'd stand out anywhere."

Suddenly, Allegra's eyes filled with tears. Toby wanted to get up and run before they spilled over, but amazingly, they didn't. They just stayed put, making the princess's eyes look bigger and darker than ever. "I just didn't know what else to do," Allegra said. "Everything has been so wonderful since I came here, and after I go back, nothing will be the same. Oh, I'll exchange letters with some of the friends I've made. And Randy and I will still care about each other for a while, but it won't last. It's all going to change and I can't bear it."

Without really thinking, Toby said, "I know Randy. And if he cares about you now,

he'll keep on caring. That won't change."
Suddenly, she stopped, realizing what she'd
just said. That Randy wouldn't stop caring
just because the princess went away.

It was true, Toby thought. Just look at the
way Randy felt about *her*. He hadn't stopped
caring about her after he met the princess.
Just tonight, when he'd been so worried, he'd
asked about Max, because he knew how much
Max meant to her.

Toby glanced at the princess and then stared
down at her hands. It had taken almost a week
of misery, but she'd finally figured it out —
Allegra didn't take Randy away from her.
Randy did. He liked her — they were special
friends — but he loved Allegra. Nothing she
could do or say or dream about was going to
change that. And here she'd wasted an entire
week feeling sorry for herself and hating the
princess when she could have been having a
good time. Randy loves Allegra — say it ten
times before you go to sleep, she told herself,
and ten more times when you wake up. Get it
through your thick skull, and then get on
with your life.

"Toby?" The princess was looking at her
curiously. "Are you all right?"

"Me?" Toby smiled. Forgetting about
Randy wasn't going to be easy, she knew, but
she'd made up her mind to do it, and making
up her mind always felt good. "I'm fine. I was
thinkin', though. This running away? It's
really a greenhorn of an idea."

Allegra started to say something, but Toby kept on talking. "For one thing, what's going to happen? Are you going to get a job someplace? Or maybe try to go to school? Do you expect Randy to drop everything — forget about his father's farm and the horses — and run to be with you? And what about your family? Somehow, I just don't think they're the kind of people who'll give up looking for you. And you're not going to be that hard to find."

Allegra opened her mouth to speak, but Toby still wasn't finished. "And another reason it's a bad idea is because I know. I tried it once." Quickly, she told the princess about her attempt to run away, and how Jane and Andy had stopped her. "If I'd gone ahead and lit out of here," she said, "I might be back at the ranch in Texas, but I'd still be runnin', in my mind. I'd still be thinking I couldn't get along with people, and that people didn't like me."

Allegra managed to jump in finally. "You're saying that the problem would have followed you."

"That's it," Toby agreed. "Now I wanted to run *back* home, and you want to run away from home, but it all comes down to the same thing — it's just running. And it doesn't get you very far."

Allegra was quiet for a long time, thinking it over. Finally, she lifted her chin, sort of like Jane did, Toby thought, when she'd decided something. "You're right, Toby," the princess said. "It was a greenhorn of an idea. Let's go back to Baker House."

Toby just nodded and began pulling on her still-wet poncho, but inside, she was really glad. Things were finally getting straightened out.

"By the way," Allegra said, as they headed for the door. "Randy told me that three sentences in a row were a big speech for you. But when you were telling me why I shouldn't run, you talked in paragraphs!"

The princess was actually grinning, and Toby couldn't help grinning back. "I don't know what came over me," she said. "I guess I just finally found the right words."

As they pushed open the door, letting in a gust of rain, the man behind the counter finally looked up. "You'll miss the bus to Pittsburgh," he said, using his thumb to save his place in the book. "It's coming in five minutes, and it won't wait."

"Thank you," Allegra told him, "But we'll have to catch it another time."

Shrugging, the man went back to his book, and the girls walked out into the rainy night. By the time the bus to Pittsburgh rolled in, Toby and Allegra were halfway back to Baker House.

The next morning, Toby woke early. Slipping out of bed, she padded over to the window to check the weather. Every leaf, branch, and flower on campus seemed to be dripping water. The grass was glistening and the old buildings looked shiny clean. But the rain had stopped and the sky was clear. It was going to be a beautiful day.

As she looked out the window, she saw Randy's pick-up come bumping up the drive to Baker House. Randy got out, went inside, and came back out with Princess Allegra. The two of them got into the truck and drove off in the direction of his farm. The two body-guards, in the limousine, followed a little way behind.

Toby turned and squinted at Jane's alarm clock. Eight o'clock. The princess was leaving at eleven, so she and Randy must have wanted to spend some time together before that.

She turned back to the window just in time to catch a glimpse of the pick-up as it curved out of sight around the building. Then she tried to figure out how she felt. The anger wasn't there anymore. The hurt was, but it wasn't nearly as bad, and she knew it would just keep getting better and better until it was completely gone.

Toby nodded to herself, satisfied that things were going to be fine. Then she turned away from the window and crossed the room to her closet. Halfway there, she tripped over a stack of books, which started to topple. She made a grab for them, lost her balance, and went sprawling onto the floor.

"I heard that," Andy said accusingly from

deep in her pillow. "If it's as early as I think it is, then it must be Toby."

"It is me," Toby said, getting to her knees. "It's dark in here. I tripped."

"You know this room is like a mine field," Andy told her. "Jane leaves little traps all over the place."

"They weren't Jane's books," Toby said sheepishly, noisily restacking the books. "They were mine."

Andy raised her head from the pillow, blinking groggily. "Don't tell me sloppiness is catching. Quick, somebody find a cure before I come down with it."

There were stirrings and mutterings from Jane's bed. "Who's sick?" she mumbled.

"Toby," Andy said, winking mischievously. "And she caught it from you."

Jane was silent for a few seconds. Then she sat straight up, staring at her two roommates. "What have I got?"

"A bad case of the sloppies," Toby said. "And it's rubbing off on me. Andy's worried she might be next."

Jane sniffed indignantly, but the others laughed until she joined in. "What are you doing up, anyway?" she asked, peering at her clock. "This is a very uncivilized hour to be awake."

"Couldn't sleep anymore," Toby said. "My stomach kept telling me to get up and feed it."

"I thought you'd sleep like a log after last night's rescue mission," Andy said.

"I did sleep like a log," Toby said. "Anyway, it wasn't a rescue mission."

"Try telling that to P.A." Andy said laughing. "She looked like she was ready to pin a medal on you."

The others laughed, too, remembering the look on Ms. Allardyce's face when Toby and the princess walked into Baker House after hours, both of them drenched with rain and laughing. The headmistress had been so relieved that she almost — but not quite — lost her poise and hugged them.

"What was so funny, anyway?" Jane asked Toby. "You two looked like you'd been in a shipwreck, but you were laughing."

"Allegra was wondering if we'd get demerit slips for being late," Toby said. "I told her probably not, seeing as how it was a special case. She was disappointed — thought a demerit slip would prove she was just a regular girl." Toby grinned. "So I said that the next time I got one, I'd be happy to send it to her."

Jane and Andy looked at each other and smiled. They couldn't help noticing the change in Toby's attitude since the day before. She was relaxed, she'd cracked a few jokes, and she was actually using words of more than one syllable. "Looks like we've got the old Toby back," Andy commented softly.

"Just about," Toby said with a smile. "Thanks, you two, for sticking with me."

"It would take more than that to get rid of us," Andy told her. "Besides, we *are* stuck —

in a good way. All three of us are stuck together."

"Stuck and starving," Jane said. "Come on, let's go to the dining hall before they have a chance to ruin breakfast!"

A little while later, the residents of 407 were back in their room, trying to recover from the fried eggs they'd eaten. "Those must have been dinosaur eggs," Andy said. "They were as hard as rocks." She started doing some sit-ups to try to hurry along the digestion process. Jane began a letter to her parents, and Toby made a pile of the books she had to return to the library later.

There was a tap on the door and Allegra came in, carrying three of Andy's blouses on hangers. "I'm bringing back the borrowed goods," she said, hanging them on a doorknob. "Thank you, Andy. They were fun to wear."

"You're welcome," Andy said. "Next time you come, I'll borrow from you!"

Allegra smiled but shook her head. "I don't think that's going to happen."

Toby looked up from the books. "You mean because you almost ran away?"

"No, because of *why* I almost ran away."

"Randy?"

Allegra nodded. "And Prince Frederick. My family's very serious about that marriage, and they're not going to be eager to let me go off again. In fact, I'm sure they'll be completely opposed."

"What are you going to do?" Jane asked.

"Go home," Allegra said. "And . . . do what they want." She sighed and then put on a bright smile. "But, I must stop complaining. I've had a wonderful time here, and I'll never forget it."

Jane and Toby nodded sympathetically, but Andy looked disgusted. "I can't believe what I'm hearing," she said. "Are we in the twentieth century or not?"

"We were the last time I heard," Toby said, slightly mystified.

"Good," Andy said, getting to her feet. "Because for a minute there, I thought we were way back in the sixteenth." Hands on her hips, she faced Allegra. "You say you want to be a normal, modern girl," she told her. "Well, a normal, modern girl doesn't let her family plan her life. If you don't want to marry the prince, or even if you just don't want to marry him *yet*, then take a stand. Fight for what you want. You might not get it, but you sure won't get it if you don't fight!"

Jane cleared her throat. "Andy believes in speaking her mind," she said, hoping Allegra wasn't offended.

"And how," Toby said.

"And she's right," Allegra said quickly. "I have been acting just like a princess in a storybook, haven't I? Weeping and wailing about how hopeless things are."

"You haven't exactly been optimistic," Andy agreed.

"Well, from now on, I plan to try," Allegra said. "But confronting my family is something I dread. I'm afraid I'll lose my nerve at the last minute and give in meekly." She thought a minute and then looked at Andy. "Would you be willing to speak your mind to me some more? In letters? If you write, I know it'll help keep my courage up."

"Sure," Andy said. "I was planning to write to you anyway. I'll just add a few extra paragraphs, cheering you on."

"Thank you," Allegra said. She checked her watch and then looked at the three roommates. "Whenever anyone asks me what's best about Canby Hall, I'll tell them about you."

Once more, girls were looking out the windows of Baker House and gathering around the front entrance. This time, they were saying good-bye, and since a lot of them had gotten to know the princess, the good-byes were much more casual than the greetings had been. Maggie gave Allegra the present everyone had contributed to — a fat candle shaped and colored like a deluxe cheeseburger.

"Does it smell like a cheeseburger when you burn it?" Andy asked.

"I hope not," Allegra laughed. "If it did, I'd be tempted to eat it!"

Joseph and Rodger hovered in the background as usual, checking their watches and waiting for the limousine. They seemed anxious to get going, as if they thought a real kidnapping might take place any minute.

Finally, the limousine pulled up. The driver got out, opened the back doors, and stood at attention. Ms. Allardyce, still looking relieved that Canby Hall hadn't been the site of a notorious crime, spoke to the princess for a minute.

Then it was time for Allegra to go. Looking around, she spotted Andy, who gave her a thumbs-up signal. Laughing, Allegra returned it, climbed into the car, and was driven away.

"Well," Toby said as the three roommates turned to go into Baker House. "That's that."

"Now what do we do?" Andy asked.

"What do you mean?" Jane said. "We'll go back to what we were doing before Allegra . . . oh, I see what you mean," she said. "I guess things will seem a little dull around here for a while."

"Right," Andy agreed. "It'll just be the same old thing."

"Maybe not," Toby said. "Maybe it won't be the same at all." She grinned and draped her arms across Jane's and Andy's shoulders. "Maybe it'll be better than ever."

Laughing in agreement, the three roommates went up the stairs to Room 407.

When a strange girl in old-fashioned clothes is seen on campus, everyone begins to wonder: Has young Julia Canby, in whose memory Canby Hall was founded so long ago, returned? Read The Girls of Canby Hall #25, THE GHOST OF CANBY HALL

Read All About
The Girls of Canby Hall!

Get ready for friends...
Get ready for fun...
Get ready for...

JUNIOR HIGH

Get ready for a fresh new year of 8th grade madness at Cedar Groves Junior High! Laugh at best friends Nora and Jen's "cool" attempts to fit in. Cringe at the exceptionally gross tricks of Jason, the class nerd. Be awed by Mia who shows up on the first day dressed in a punk outfit. And meet Denise, "Miss Sophistication," who shocks Nora and Jen by suggesting they invite *BOYS* to the Halloween party!

Get ready for JUNIOR HIGH, a new series about the funny side of life in junior high school.

Look for these new Junior High titles at your nearest bookstore!
$2.25 U.S./$2.95 CAN.

JUNIOR HIGH JITTERS #1 by M.L. Kennedy

CLASS CRUSH #2 by Kate Kenyon

**THE DAY THE EIGHTH GRADE
RAN THE SCHOOL #3** by Kate Kenyon

HOW DUMB CAN YOU GET? #4 by Kate Kenyon

JH873